BREATH OF LIFE

Collected Works

L.H. MOORE

ISBN (Print) 978-1-955765-29-9

Cover art by Paul Lewin

Jacket Design by Mikio Murakami

Apex Book Company

Lexington, KY, USA

Visit us online at https://www.apexbookcompany.com.

For Socky

Thank you Ancestors

CONTENTS

Roots On Ya — 1

Breath of Life — 9

A Little Not Music — 19

A Clink of Crystal Glasses Heard — 34

Here, Kitty — 44

Hidden — 55

Empty Vessel — 56

What Was THAT?! — 66

VOX — 70

A Place Called Home — 72

With These Hands: A Tale of Uncommon Labour — 78

Rule of Thirds — 88

Peregrination — 98
(Co-written with Chesya Burke)

On Vision and Audacity — 126

Publication Information — 129

About the Author — 131

ROOTS ON YA

1906, Louisa County, Virginia

I was there when the things came up out of her.

The girl—Maddie and 'em's youngest named Heddy—choked and gagged them right out of herself, retching long and loud. Beetles and bugs and even a small black garter snake wriggled its way on through. All them things fell on the ground writhing and scuttling away. She had on this nice yellow dress since, after all, we was at a get-together. It didn't stay nice for long with that black mess spewing out all over. Everyone else just stood there in their Sunday best looking on with their mouths open, their eyes wide. Some of the ladies hollered. One fainted dead away. Even the menfolk gasped and let loose an *Oh Lord* here and there.

Me? I just sighed.

A big, long, deep, *deep* sigh.

I done seen some things.

I know I wasn't even flinching. Maybe not even blinking twice. My eyes went heavenward for a moment right when that poor gal's tear-streaked ones fixed on mine, all scared and pleading. Just as she tried to say something to me, her stomach started heaving again.

Heddy's dark brown hand went to cover her mouth, only for her to snatch it away, recoiling as more of the same poured out. All I could think was, *What has one of y'all gone and done now?*

"Lawd, Reely, you just gonna stand there and let this happen to my baby?!" Maddie, the girl's mother hollered, her round face hysterical as her daughter alternately screamed and gagged.

"Aw hell ... *Fine then,*" I said, breaking the moment of whatever was going on there with all of these folks. "It's not like I'd just let her be like that." Wouldn't take me too long to run home, and I got to go now after what else I'm seeing lurking.

It's one of them. Aw no.

Not one of them.

Something was really, really off. "Make her as comfortable as you can. I'll go and get my things."

We are so glad you hear. Our voices are not stilled.
We are so glad you listen. You know to trust our words.
We are so glad you learned. This knowledge is now yours, too.
Use it well, use it right, use it well.

Just happened to be that I had a notion of how this one started: Li'l Miss Gal in Yellow—Heddy—liked that Gillis boy way too much for Millie's—Harris and Mabel's gal's—liking. So, that Millie probably got ahold of some of her hair and baked it in a cake. Wonder she ain't go mute too. Probably got some of that gal's water too, dabbling around in things she shouldn't have without no protection. If she knew better, she could've just gone on and tried to get that boy direct—a little blood of hers go a long way. Least I hope she didn't. Lawd only knows what kind of crossing Millie done put on that poor Heddy, but she was now hacking up her insides and then some. I got to get it off her. I ain't got much time.

Things ain't right here at all. I studied the faces of everyone there as I tried to figure out what had me so unsettled, like something creeping all along the edges of my senses. The Gillis boy stood there like all the others, a look of disgust and fascination on his face. Standing next to him as close to him as she could be—and with the *nerve* to be smiling—was that Millie.

I caught her eye.

She caught mine and looked away.

Wouldn't have bothered me or nobody else as we weren't the one she was aiming for, but I ain't eat none of that cake she made. It was all lemony and moist-looking (I hate some dry cake), but nah ... I don't eat nothing at these get-togethers anyway. All of 'em know me and they all know why and the reason why I got to be extra careful with mine. I make my own food. Hunt and raise my own critters. Grow my own plants. If I got to be out, I pack my meal or I ain't eating 'til I get back. Rest of them just laugh about it, but I know that kind of laughter. They laugh a li'l higher. They smile a li'l broader. You can see it in the nervous way their eyes move when they do. That's laughing that's got a bit of fear about it.

Like it's funny only 'cause they feel they *better* laugh.

Sometimes you hear us walking 'round ...
Sometimes talking upon the breeze.
You often hear us singing,
A chorus you join with ease.

I hurried over to my horse Rufus, who whinnied as I approached. I patted his russet-colored head and hopped up onto the saddle. You'll usually never find me without some basics like my oils and water in my satchel today, but this? This is something else. I needed to go home.

I sang to myself as we galloped along the dirt roads back to my place in Apple Grove. I go to church and my family always has and does, but I ain't much for it. Love singing the spirituals, though. "You got a good strong voice there, Reely," Lettie said to me the other Sunday, looking at me with those beautiful brown eyes of hers. She could tell me that the Sun goes 'round the Earth and I'd believe her. I'd walk on air and breathe water like a fish if she thought I could.

I clucked my tongue at Rufus, urging him to go faster. I've helped everyone around these parts at some point, from babies to the elders. Sometimes it's just small ailments. Sometimes it's bad things like this. Every time's different. I just listen to what they tell me and remember what I know.

Passed some of my neighbors walking along the roads who waved at me as we rushed by. Rufus and I turned sharply and cut through the woods. I could ride this route in the pitch-black at this point if need be. We popped out through the treeline and rode right up to my place. I tied Rufus up, gave him some water, and made my way towards the door.

My frizzy hen out front started clucking and scratching furiously when she saw me, ruffling up dark feathers speckled with white spots like so many stars. My daddy told me these birds came on over from in Africa like us. Got those special gifts like us, too. I petted her and softly said "I know, girly, I know ... scratch them bad roots right on up. That conjure got to go and it can't go up in here. Gotta be careful." A wooden bucket sat beside the door. I lifted the lid, looking at the green and brown herbs swirling on the water's surface inside. Took the gourd and splashed some of it over my doorstep, before grabbing the broom that sat next to it and sweeping the front. I reached into a little tin in my satchel and sprinkled some salt and cayenne pepper around my footsteps and at the doorway. "This mess just gonna stay on out here with you, hen. You and Them know what to do."

I opened my door and stepped inside. My place is real simple. Built it myself. Just a small log home. One big large comfortable room. Got a table, a bed and two chairs. One for me and one for guests 'cause ain't nobody just gonna be sitting up on my bed all like that. There's a cellar and even got a secret way out besides the front door. Ain't telling how. Wouldn't be a secret then. But see? Real simple.

I always look around first. Make sure no one's been up in here. I can feel it beforehand any way, but I ain't trying to come home into no surprises. I got two rifles and the spirits by my side.

I'd be ready.

Went over to my shelf and got a bowl. Checked out and picked up different jars with herbs and powders up in them. The drying herbs hanging up around me filled the place with their fragrance. It's all as familiar as breathing to me. I quickly got a fire going and set a small pot out to boil. I kinda mutter to myself when I'm doing this. Talking through it all. Helps me focus. Helps me hear. Making sure I got the right stuff. One thing might heal, but mixed with something else'll kill quicker than anything.

I put the ingredients into my mortar and pestle and crushed it all up. Got a clean white cloth to strain it through into a flask. Also bundled some more herbs together and put them into a small pouch. Said the prayer over it that my daddy taught me and his momma before him. I gotta get back to Heddy and whatever it was I saw going on there. Secured my place again and ran over to Rufus, hopping onto him with a leap.

Now you know this is for good
Now you know the things you should
When you use the gift for bad
The Others hear...don't make them mad.

Once again, Rufus and I galloped through the Virginia countryside. I could see the crowd still gathered there as the white, clapboard church came into view. Everyone's heads turned in unison as I rode down right at them, slowing Rufus down and handing his reins over to whoever was near.

"Lawd, Lawd, LAWD, have mercy on this girl! In the name of ..." Pastor Lee was standing there praying over Heddy, now curled up on the ground surrounded by the black mess. Her hair was mussed and she was still screaming and crying and holding her stomach.

Pastor Lee's lips pursed together tightly as I approached, but even he stepped back. He raised his hands in the air, the full sleeves of his black robe catching the breeze as he loudly declared "God Bless Brother Aurelius as he helps this poor child. Let the Lord work wond'rous things through him!" I shook my head, somewhat amused, but figured this girl could use all the extra blessings that she could get. They all gave me a whole lot of space as I knelt down beside her.

I placed a hand across her forehead, closing my eyes and concentrating before pulling out the flask I had filled. My hand began to feel warm, with heat radiating in pulses to my now tingling fingertips. She felt like she was swirling inside. I dropped back in my mind to that place where I could try to gather it, contain it. I could feel it fighting me, fighting back, its dark tendrils trying to creep out and touch me, but nah, I thought ... I got ya. *I got ya.* I pushed forth, wrapping it like a bundle with golden twine, crunching it down, and forcing it to be quiet.

I got ya.

I said an invocation in a low voice and asked Heddy's ancestors to come forth. I felt a wave sweep past and through me. "I know y'all are here. She can't call you herself right now. Help her out like I know only you can, please." An older man and a younger woman appeared beside her, in shades of shimmering gray. They both nodded and smiled at me as they each placed a hand on her. "C'mon now gal ... drink some of this. It probably ain't gonna taste too good, but it's going to get it out. C'mon now, it'll be alright. Let me help you." I held the flask to her blackened, ooze-stained lips as she took her first sip. As I expected, she gagged a little, making a face of disgust. "Go on. Ain't no worse than what you done already coughed out." Her momma shot me a withering look.

Heddy drained the flask. Her retching started to subside and then finally stopped. She leaned against her momma, who had also knelt down beside her. I told her to watch Heddy until the next day and handed her the cloth pouch filled with my selection of herbs.

"Brew this up and make sure she bathes in it. Pour it over her head too and let her air dry. Gotta clean her out. Get rid of this mess. All of it."

"Oh, thank you Brother Reely! Thank you! What can we do for you?"

"Well, there's nothing you can give me food-wise..."

Maddie stopped and stared at me. "You ain't right sometimes, you know?" I shrugged and started to say something right on back to her, but noticed the ancestors hadn't left yet. One of them was motioning towards something. I nodded.

Hovering nearby was that gal Millie who put the trick on Heddy in the first place. I saw her and shot her a look letting her know I did. She wasn't smiling as much anymore. As Heddy got better and the spectacle had stopped, the crowd broke off, leaving to go home after all of the excitement. I stood up, people pausing as I pointed directly at the one who did the crossing.

"Hey there gal," I said loudly. The heads of everyone present turned to look at her in unison as her eyes went wide. "You. Yes, *you*. Ya might wanna stop for a minute so I can tell you that everything comes with a price and you're messing with something that messes back."

Murmurs and "Nuh-uhs" swept through the crowd, their voices becoming louder as my words sank in. I saw Lettie in the crowd and was relieved that she had on the necklace that I gave her for protection. The Gillis boy looked at Millie with disgust and backed away as she shrank from the crowd's accusations and admonishments. See, thing is, whole time I could see something they couldn't...this tall dark shadow that was with her, just behind her. Everywhere she was moving, it was moving, too. I recognized it for what it was and knew that anywhere that she would go, it would go, too. It wasn't just her being obvious (at least to me) about what she did to that other gal that made me notice her. It was that Other that was now with her. I had already seen it earlier just standing there smiling.

Smiling at *me*.

"Yeah, I see ya." I say to it. "Gal, you gone and done it. If you gonna do a crossing, do it right and sure as hell don't let it stay with you like this."

The Other shifted behind her, laughing.

"Oh, you laughing, huh?" I shook my head and sighed. A long, deep sigh knowing that I am never finished.

I DONE SEEN SOME THINGS.

BREATH OF LIFE

1858, Futa Toro, Senegambia

Forward is the only way, and it is often without a clear path, Oumar thought as he smoothed out a small piece of paper. He was focused as he wrote an inscription upon it, his script careful and deliberate. He carefully creased each fold before gently tucking it into a small brown leather pouch. After saying a prayer over it, he handed it to the woman who sat across from him, her eyes downcast in a face that was worried and drawn.

"You have suffered so much already. This should help you," he said as she started to thank him profusely. "Salaam aleikum. May peace be with you." The woman's dark brown hands were shaking as she quickly tied it around her waist and hurried out.

He could hear the sound of women outside pounding millet with large wooden pestles, the rhythmic thumps complemented by their singing. *Perhaps things are finally returning to normal.* Picking up his reed pen, Oumar dipped it into the ink and started to write again. He looked up as one of the students from his Qu'ranic school came to the doorway.

"Excuse me, Teacher," the small boy said, swatting away a pesky fly that landed on his face. "The *almami* and the council of elders want to see you."

"Thank you." The boy ran off to join his friends as Oumar carefully set aside the prayer sheets and papers he had been creating—their white surfaces covered with the black ink of his precise writing and geomantic drawings filled with graphs and symbols. After he rolled up the reed mat he was sitting on, Oumar looked around his simple dwelling with its thatched roof and mud brick walls. A bowl of millet couscous with groundnut leaf sauce sat waiting, as well as a calabash of milk left for him by the woman he'd made the gris-gris talisman for earlier. Small wooden boards with verses from the Qu'ran that had been prepared for his students were neatly stacked against a wall and he thought about his lessons and how school had been interrupted lately. An ornately carved wooden chest in the corner caught his eye and he sighed as he looked at it.

This was inevitable. He stood up and straightened his robes and the fabric that hung loosely about his shoulders.

I am the only one now.

❧

"OUMAR BA, WE ARE SURE THAT YOU KNOW WHY YOU ARE HERE," the *almami* said. A reed-thin Toucouleur noble whose Arab heritage was evident by his features and light red-brown skin, Dényanké was leader of their village. Although he was the foremost person to take action on behalf of it, the elders actually governed and were consulted on all major matters. They scrutinized Oumar as he entered the room and took a seat before them. They sat silently in front of him with folded arms, their embroidered robes neatly falling in deep folds around them. Many had been friends of his father and grandfather and he could see that all of their eyes registered doubt.

They must have faith. They must.

"Do you believe that you can overcome it?" Dényanké asked.

"What are our other options? What other hope do we have for ourselves? For *them?*" Oumar said as he waved his hands towards the people gathered outside the doorway that were straining to hear. "This thing is an abomination. It is an upset to *baraka* and an affront to Allah. It is not intent on contributing to the breath of life if all it will bring is death. I suppose that is why I must go after it. Who else *can?*"

"You are right," one of the elders said sadly. "There is no one else left but you now."

Dényanké's face looked grim as Oumar got up to leave. "May Allah be with you—and all of us."

Oumar walked back to his home, followed by children and villagers shouting out to him in support. As he stepped inside, he found his apprentice Bayo sitting there writing, startled by all of the noise. Bayo looked past him at the crowd of people as he quickly put his work aside.

"Teacher, I hope you do not mind my presence right now. I thought I'd take care of some things while I had the chance," he said. "I take it the Council made its decision."

"Yes, and I am asking you to come with me. I will need you, starting with your help in getting prepared for the journey."

Oumar and Bayo went around his home gathering supplies for the trip. Oumar walked over to the wooden chest—its golden accents gleaming—and opened it, fingering the papers and contents inside. His fingers tingled as he touched the cover of a well-worn copy of the Qu'ran handwritten by his grandfather.

This is it, my ancestors. All you have taught me has led to this.

May Allah watch over us all.

AS THEY PREPARED TO LEAVE THE VILLAGE, OUMAR LOOKED ahead into the distance. He slowly walked ahead with his head held high, but his soul was heavy with the weight of the entire village's expectations pinned on him and him alone. In hindsight, Oumar thought that perhaps his statement may have been too cocky, too bold, too presumptuous.

For hours and hours they walked through the countryside, only stopping to rest and eat a little dried mutton from their bags and ripe mangoes from the trees. He squinted as the sun started to lower in the sky, causing the baobabs with their twisted, gnarled branches to cast dark shadows across the ground. He thought of the griots—the keepers of oral history, legend and song—who were often entombed within their hollow cores. He could feel the essence of those old trees as they passed, each one strongly pulsing with the heartbeat of the land—reminding him of the millet pounding of the women.

The only person who had been willing to go with him on this hunt for the rogue djinn was Bayo, whose tall, lanky frame looked as if it had been swallowed by his long white tunic and loose slacks. Only his eyes were visible beneath the white fabric wound around his head and face and they nervously darted from side to side. As the men made their way through the dry savannah grasses and sand, Bayo's fear was almost palpable. The young man shifted the leather satchel on his shoulder before turning to look at his mentor.

"Are we really going to do what you said when we find it?" he asked, turning and brushing against the billowing white fabric of Oumar's voluminous outer robes.

"Yes. We shall talk," Oumar said.

"Talk? What if it will not reason? *If* it is capable of that. Then what?"

"If there is no reason—no compromise—then we will resort to our original plan. As for right now, all we can do is continue to wait." Bayo didn't look too convinced as he joined Oumar—who squatted in the thick peach-colored sand—and prepared to begin his prayers. When they finished, Oumar sat with his hands folded in his lap. His calm demeanor was in sharp contrast to how he actually felt—a little anxious about coming face-to-face with the scourge of their small village.

Oumar thought more about his task as he walked. A djinn. Not an angel, yet not a demon. Moving with the whirlwinds and whims of the desert sands, they could be mischievous one moment and spiteful the next. Yet, this one was different. It was unusual for a djinn to create the kind of havoc that had been unleashed in Oumar's village.

Too many times now had screams awakened him during the night, everyone shrieking at once as they rushed out to find chaos in the aftermath. The other villagers ran around frantically as women whirled in place howling with grief as they clutched their children close to them. Even grown men cried out in horror as the corpses and body parts of loved ones, friends and neighbors were found scattered across the ground like petals. Oumar knew this carnage meant only one thing:

It had returned.

Oumar winced just thinking about it. In the light of morning, he would reflect upon how the attacks seemed to happen so fast that even he was unable to feel or predict them coming. That was something that had never happened before. Amid the grief-stricken cries and wails from bereaved relatives, the dead—who had been mutilated and torn into pieces during the night—were properly put to rest, leaving those left behind with a choice they did not want to have.

"What will we do?" they all asked him as one by one they came to him for some form of protection—anything to comfort them against this unknown. "What *can* we do?"

Oumar contemplated everything he knew—reflecting upon the fact that he had probably been in training for a time like this all of his life, although he had hoped it wouldn't come to something like this. For years he studied the mysticism of his Tijaniyya Sufi sect at Qu'ranic school under the disciplined tutelage under his father and grandfather—both powerful marabouts and leaders in their faith. With them both now gone, it was up to him to help his people.

He knew he was only one in a long line of Toucouleur marabouts and female seers. His ancestors had been among the first to help spread Islam in their region, yet even so, some of the ancient mystical ways still remained as well. So far he had shown the village only a sampling of the special things that he could do, but this time would be the ultimate test.

Oumar had been told the stories of the Unseen One and had believed them to be just children's bogeyman tales until his grandfather brought him the scrolls. Oumar had gasped as he looked upon the ancient records written in a fading hand that documented their village being preyed upon for centuries. That which had once been but a story he now knew to be very real. Oumar felt it was his duty to try to defend his village the best way he knew how.

He was now ready to negotiate with it—or battle it once and for all.

"Bayo, while we still have some light, let us do as we planned." The apprentice opened the satchel and handed him the paper shirts, drawings, and amulets from within.

"Teacher, are you wearing the amulet that I made for you as well?" Bayo asked eagerly, as Oumar reached up and fingered the small bone and leather pendant around his neck that he had been wearing lately. "I made it myself and I was hoping you still had it on."

"I am, thank you. I'll take whatever extra protection I can get." Omar said, as they both rushed to put everything on under their robes. The two of them worked quickly to prepare the area around them as well, arranging the papers under the sand in a circle. The two of them surveyed their work, pleased.

As he and Bayo sat in the center and waited, the sun finally dipped even lower—throwing a spectrum of color over the dry, yellow-tan brush that stretched as far as they could see. Oumar could see the gleaming silver ribbon of the river in the distance as they sat in expectation.

"How do you know it will come?" Bayo said with a hint of resignation.

"It will come because it is tired. It will come because it is time."

"And you are *certain* of this?" Bayo asked again with a long sigh as the last orange glow of the sun started to dissipate along the horizon.

"It will. Quiet now."

In the silence that followed, Oumar closed his eyes and relaxed—allowing himself to meditate and concentrate on everything around him. With a flash of white, he felt his mind open up. He felt weightless in the void as it filtered through all of the stimuli. From the sound of Bayo's rapid heartbeat to the feel of the weight of the air itself, he allowed himself to be open to the universe—including its more unsavory occupants. A faint thin smell came to him. Its rank, rancid, fetid scent was growing stronger and stronger.

It is coming.

It was immense, and almost stifling in its anger and animosity as it came rushing towards them with startling speed. Oumar could feel it—ancient, unstable, unsure of his intent. Almost as soon as he had picked up on these impressions, the presence was before them.

Its voice—a low and guttural growl—came to him within his head before he actually saw it. He opened his eyes to see Bayo still sitting beside him. The djinn's attention shifted.

"You have no quarrel with him, Old One," Oumar politely told it in a calm, even voice. Bayo looked up, fear filling his face, but did as instructed beforehand by trying to remain calm.

Oumar could now see the djinn clearly with the disappearance of the sun. Tall, yet thin of build, the Old One was appearing to him as a man. Gaunt, with long, razor-sharp fingernails, it turned its milky, luminescent eyes upon them. The dust had started to settle around the djinn as it stopped moving, but its gray, bloodied robes flowed around it in undulating tattered rags as if still propelled by the whirlwind. Its forearms were covered with blood and thick, crusting gore. Oumar watched in barely contained disgust as the djinn licked blood away from its ashen lips, exposing sharp, fanged teeth.

"I see you are not surprised by my appearance," the Old One said, his voice now a series of rumbles like that of a storm passing.

"With all due respect, I am not here to comment on your looks. I am here to discuss, to negotiate with you."

"You? Negotiate with *me*? That is laughable," the Old One said in contempt as his milky eyes looked at Oumar. "It will not happen. I am owed as much for what was done to me so long ago."

"So long ago that it has faded into memory? Old One, let it blow away like this dust we now stand upon. You must let go of your past and need for revenge. Be absolved. Move forward and contribute to the universal energy once more. There is no need to continue down this wicked path."

"Never again. This is of my choosing."

"This is your wish?"

"It is," it said, taking a step towards them.

"Not one step more," Bayo said, pointing towards the ground for emphasis. "Not one step."

"Oh, he speaks I see?"

"Bayo? You can see it?" Oumar said, his pride in his apprentice's awareness swelling just as the djinn moved swiftly, creating a strong breeze that shifted the dirt around it, exposing a paper mat with inscriptions. Angered, it turned and stood before him. Oumar blanched at the djinn's discovery of his ruse.

It whirled around, its teeth bared. "How <u>dare</u> you try to trick me and bind me!"

Oumar stepped back, shocked that it did not work. *How could that be?* The djinn used this surprise to its advantage, advancing upon him with one hand raised—its claws menacing.

"Now my teacher! NOW!" Bayo shouted, distracting the djinn for a moment, just long enough for Oumar to get his bearings and start to recite supplications to Allah. At that moment, the djinn paused on another of his geomantic papers that had been hidden under the sand.

The djinn screeched—a deafening piercing howl—and its body lurched forward before jerking backwards again as if pulled by marionette strings. Despite its convulsions, Oumar's body started to chill and prickle all over as he felt the djinn building up the strength to combat all of their work by draining energy from the space around it. It looked at Oumar one more time before sneering and moving towards Bayo.

"NO!" Oumar yelled as the djinn rapidly closed in on his apprentice. Bayo screamed, his eyes closed as the djinn approached. It took one swipe at the young man, who cried out in pain as the djinn's talons cut into his flesh, tearing through his clothes and paper shirt before it abruptly disappeared. He turned around, looking for what he still sensed was there.

Where did it go? I can feel its essence, but where could it have gone?

Oumar caught his breath and turned to look at Bayo. He was surprised to see his apprentice standing before him with a large rock in his hands. Confusion spread across Oumar's face. "Bayo! What are you *doing?*"

Bayo's face was contorted with a delirious, feverish pleasure.

Oh, no.

Oumar's eyes widened with a comprehending realization and his hands flew to the amulet around his neck. The amulet! He had been deceived. Bayo had learned from him a little *too* well—including blocking Oumar's abilities when it came to this djinn. His mind raced as he thought of the village and its people ... how they would be picked off one by one...

Everything around him blurred in his panic as Bayo suddenly brought the stone down upon him. He felt blood streaming from the side of his head, and once again started to recite the supplications, repeating them over and over again, hoping the effect of the powerful words would help him. Oumar's voice sounded slurred and thick to himself as he began to lose consciousness. As his eyes started to close, he could see the djinn reappear beside Bayo, its sharp teeth curving into a smile as it raised one of its claw-like hands again. Oumar felt searing pain as it started to rip into him.

"I knew you would come," Bayo said to it, smiling as Oumar's body crumpled forward to the ground.

"I knew my master would come for me."

A LITTLE NOT MUSIC

1939, Washington, D.C.

Alice looped her arm through that of her best friend Bea, their infectious laughter making the people they passed by smile as they walked down the street. "U Street! Black Broadway!" Alice declared out loud, throwing her free arm out dramatically as Bea hip-bumped her. "This is where *everyone* wants to be!"

The bars, clubs, theaters, and cabarets were hopping that night, like every night, their marquees and signs bright. Posters announced upcoming acts. Folks dressed to the nines in flashy furs drove shiny flashy cars. Everybody was out: numbers runners, laughing college students like themselves, stumbling drunks, couples out on the town. See and be seen. The energy was crackling all around them and Alice loved being a part of that. They stopped in front of the little restaurant where Bea served as a hostess, its orange neon sign blinking overhead. "This is me," she said, her smile broad in her dark brown face. Bea adjusted her hat, a smart little number with a net veil, as she opened the door. "You knock 'em dead tonight!"

"And you know the truth! Don't I always, darling?" Alice said before waving goodbye and making her way a few doors down. There was a crowd out in front of Club Crystal Caverns as always, clamoring to get in or hoping for a peek at a celebrity that may have come through that night. She sashayed effortlessly by them as the door was opened for her with a flourish by the club's bouncer Jimmy, who greeted her with a nod as he tried to corral the eager group outside. She turned in a different direction than the clubgoers, making her way downstairs towards the back.

Backstage was always hectic before a show. She took off her hat, undoing a few pin curls she had hidden underneath. Alice and the five other dancers were a flurry of fringe, sequins, and makeup powder in their small dressing room. Shouts rang back and forth between them all and their harried assistant, who helped them dress and handled small crises. Alice stashed her bag after she squeezed into her costume and did her makeup. She got a chance to take a breath and looked around the room at the other dancers. Their spangled, sparkling costumes were all different variations on how much skin the management felt they could get away with showing in a respectable establishment. Alice had been self-conscious the first time she wore it and still adjusted her costume to make sure that what needed to be covered stayed that way. She made sure to tie the ribbon of her low-heeled tap shoes with a bow right in the center. She tapped her foot a few times to make sure it felt right.

Management also insisted that there were certain things they could do to look similar to one another. Physically they looked alike anyway with all of them being fairer in complexion and small in height. Before she had more time to muse on that fact Alice heard the stage manager call to them. She stooped down so that one of the other dancers could help her put on one of the elaborate head-dresses that they were all wearing that night. The dancers nodded and smiled at one another as they lined up, a mix of palpable anxiety and excitement, any rivalries set aside for the moment as they got ready to entertain. *All those years that my parents paid for dancing lessons have finally come in handy*, she thought wryly as one by one they went out onto the stage.

Alice could feel the *thump thump thump* of the music beneath her feet as they went through their routine, hips shimmying and feet tapping on the wooden dance floor. No matter how many times she had done this, it always felt the same—electric. The band behind them were pure energy: the frenetic flying fingers of the pianist, the blaring of the horns as their players swung them in unison, the *bom bom bom* of the bass, and the drummer setting the pace for them all. As she raised her arms, she was glad for her petite size as the club's low ceiling was stuccoed and formed to look like an underground cave grotto, with faux stalactites always a misjudged arm swing away.

Alice could see the audience out there, light glinting from their glasses as Washington's Black elite were dressed in their finest, swilling champagne and laughing and clapping as they sat at small, round, white linen tables. She could see them smiling and didn't care what anyone thought of her—or her skimpy outfit—when she danced. She whirled and kicked and found herself smiling back.

Dancing felt like freedom.

It was late when Alice got back to the house, a pale green and white-painted Victorian on a side street near school. She tried to be as quiet as possible as she made her way upstairs to her little rented room. It was a simple space, spare yet cozy, but it was hers and her own little haven from the world. As she started changing into her nightclothes, she noticed her window was still open and walked over to it. She moved one of the light cotton curtains aside and saw movement in the backyard, as if something darted across quickly. *What was THAT?!* she thought in alarm as she squinted, peering out to see what was there. *Nothing. There's nothing there. Probably just some animal or something. I'm too tired for this mess.* She closed the shades and turned around, practically falling into her bed with exhaustion.

Just as she started to drift off, Alice could hear music. She lay there for a moment listening. *Bom bom bom* went the bass with a tinny-sounding piano tinkling away. A simple, old blues song. Alice opened her eyes and looked around. It didn't sound far away enough to be neighbors having a party. It sounded like it was coming from inside the house. She knew that Bea liked to play music sometimes, but turned it off late night so that Alice and Miss Clara, the older woman who owned the house, could get some rest. The music stopped almost as abruptly as it started. *What in the world?* She was now wide awake, listening intently and trying to figure out what just happened. There was a loud creak on the side of her bed and it felt as if it was being pressed down by someone at her side.

"Pay attention," a low male voice said breathily right at her left ear, startling Alice so much that she recoiled and jumped away from it in the opposite direction, almost falling out of the small, iron-railed bed. *What WAS that?!* She had even felt the voice's vibration. She sat upright, frozen in place as she gripped the bedcovers. Her eyes darted back and forth, knowing that the room was empty except for herself. She quickly contemplated her options: *Should I run out? Should I wake up Bea and Miss Clara? What just happened here?!* She looked around in the dim of her room again. There was nothing there. No one and nothing. *There's nothing here, that wasn't real, there's nothing here*, she told herself as she tried to calm back down. She slid back down under the covers, still jittery and unnerved.

There was no sleep for her that night.

❧❧

IN THE MORNING, ALICE FINALLY DRIFTED DOWNSTAIRS, WHERE Bea was sitting at the dining room table eating a biscuit with some scrambled eggs. "Mmph, mmph, *mmph!*" Bea said as she took another bite, smiling at the gray-haired woman sitting at the table's head. "Miss Clara, you really outdid yourself with these today!" Bea's dark hair was shiny, her curls neatly in place. She patted the side of her head touching them as she turned and looked at Alice. "Ooo, girl, I'm so excited! I can't wait for my beau to come up here from school tonight!"

"If all goes well, maybe you'll be Mrs. Dr. Johnson someday," Alice said, her smile more subdued than normal.

Bea squealed with delight at the thought. "I'm telling you, he's going to be such a good one! He's staying with his friends instead of..." She stopped talking and raised an arched eyebrow at her friend. "Wait ... Alice, you seem a little worse for wear this morning. Are you alright?"

Alice averted her eyes for a moment before responding. "I thought I heard a man's voice in the middle of the night. Right in my ear, but there was no one there. No one there at all and everyone was asleep. Scared me pretty good."

This time it was Miss Clara's turn to raise an eyebrow. "Girl, that must've been some dream. Don't you go on talking about haints and such. You know I don't like that kind of mess in my home."

"But Miss Clara, I swear it happened. I'm not crazy or anything."

"Mmm-hm," Miss Clara said, unconvinced. "What you *are* crazy about is working at that club. What is a respectable girl like you doing working in a place like that?" She shook her head as she handed Alice a plate.

"My job is just a tap dancer. I show up, I dance, I get my money for school and life. Nothing more. No sense in letting all those lessons go to waste. It is paying for my tuition. Just a means to an end."

"Besides, Miss Clara," Bea interjected with a smile as she tried to change the subject. She shot a look across the table at Alice. "All of the big time jazz stars come and play there: Duke, Pearl, Cab, Ella ... it's the place to be! You should go see for yourself." Miss Clara just shook her head again.

"I think not. Something about that place, that's all," she said with a sniff as she finished her breakfast and went into the kitchen, leaving the two younger women behind. Alice leaned over the table a little towards Bea, whispering.

"I'm telling you, I definitely heard a man."

Bea looked a little nervous for a moment. "Know that I believe you, hon. If you say you heard it, you heard it." They ate the rest of their breakfast in silence.

❧

THUMP, THUMP, THUMP WENT THE MUSIC AND ALICE TAPPED HER foot to the beat as they waited backstage. She closed her eyes for a moment, letting the rhythm carry her for a moment as she prepared for her performance. Except this time, it was tempered by her fatigue. For many nights now Alice had been sleeping fitfully, her dreams always the same. She would be standing in a room so dim she could not see her hands before her. Always she would try to feel around her hoping for a door or way out into the light again, but there was nothing but empty, nothing to touch. A tall, dim shadow always lurked along the wall, always speaking with the low, butter-smooth voice from before. He had finally told her to call him The Mentor. She sighed out loud as she thought about the dreams, thinking about the senselessness of them and her situation in general. The Mentor was ever present in them both with a voice like a little menacing serenade.

She opened her eyes again wearily and stood up straight, adjusting her costume and putting on a smile before following the dancer ahead of her out into the lights and the small stage floor. Her smile faded almost as soon as they began their routine and she looked out into the audience. *What is going on? Something isn't right.* Her eyes widened in disbelief when she saw liquid dripping from the ceiling and stalactites down onto the clubgoers below. *Thump, thump, thump.* They continued to laugh and smile and chat as they always did, but the thick, viscous liquid was rolling down their heads and faces, coating their carefully coiffed hair, staining their fine clothes and furs, and pooling on the white linen tablecloths. Drops fell into their drinks, turning them red, and Alice recoiled as they sipped from them.

Blood, she thought as she gasped. *That is blood.*

Bewildered by what she was seeing, Alice lost the beat and stumbled into the dancer to her left, who shot her a confused, annoyed look. She recovered quickly, jumping back into step in sync with her colleagues. They tapped and kicked and swung their arms as Alice tried not to focus on what she was seeing out there. *Oh God, oh God...is no one else seeing this?*

Thump, thump, thump.

Then she saw *him*. The Mentor stood there in the back corner of the room, leaning against the wall with his arms crossed watching her. Silhouetted from the light of the doorway behind him, he looked as he did in her dreams: tall, formless yet with form, a shadow yet solid, everything dark. This time was different—she met his eyes, or the dark spaces where eyes should have been, and The Mentor threw back his head and laughed, his white teeth glinting in the low light as he pointed a slender hand at her. Alice lost her step again and froze in panic before running off the stage. Her colleagues stopped for only a moment to watch her leave before picking up their routine once more.

Thump, thump, thump.

A FEW DAYS LATER, ALICE WAS IN HER ROOM SURROUNDED BY HER books and notes studying for an exam. When the house was still, it was just her and the nighttime city sounds. Since she saw *him*, what used to bring her calm now made her nervous and being able to hear things so well in the quiet of the evening troubled her instead. She felt really lucky that the club didn't can her for running offstage like that and she was still rattled from her experience. Management gave her another chance and bought her excuse that she had not been feeling very well that night, which was not entirely untrue. "You're a good girl and a good dancer," management told her. "We'll cut you a break this time, but that can't happen again or you're out." She sighed at the thought, her lip curling up at the memory, and leaned back onto the pillows, careful not to dislodge the scarf around her carefully pinned up hair. She was beginning to think that her mind was slipping. *Maybe school or work is too stressful and working on me?* There was a loud knock on her door. She sat up suddenly, surprised, and got up to get it, unsure if she had somehow missed Bea or Miss Clara while lost in her thoughts. She opened it and no one was there. As she peeked out, a look of confusion crossed her face as she looked up and down the hall. No one was there. The door clicked as she slowly closed it behind her, shaking her head.

I'm letting this get to me. Maybe I was hearing things?

She settled back down on her bed and started reading again. This time, Alice could clearly hear the familiar sound of Miss Clara's soft footsteps starting down the hallway. Alice did not think much of it. *She must have left something downstairs.* Suddenly a voice was right in her ear. "Made you look!" it said in a low hiss, before it let out a harsh, raspy laugh, obviously amused with itself. She dropped her book, jumped out of bed and ran towards the center of the room. *The Mentor.* "Stop this!" Alice called out as she looked around in the room's dim light. His laughter had barely faded when she heard a scream and a series of hard bumps as if something was falling. *Thump, thump, thump.* It stopped with a loud thud. Alice threw open her door and ran out of her room to the top of the stairs. "Oh my God!" she said as she rushed down to Miss Clara, who was lying in a heap at the bottom crying out in pain.

Bea was soon at their side, her face still slathered with night cream and her hair also pinned and tied up. Her robe was tied loosely as they both hovered over Miss Clara. "I'll get an ambulance," Bea said, running to the telephone on the wall nearby. Alice could hear her talking to the operator as she tried to comfort Miss Clara, who was a bit beside herself. "No worries," she told her. "They'll be here soon."

Alice stayed with her when the ambulance came. Miss Clara was still a little shaken as she sat there later at Freedman's Hospital wringing her hands over and over again. "Doctors say that I broke my foot. I'm telling you that I thought I felt a hand upon my back push me hard as I was going downstairs," she said. "But that can't be. It was just me there. That could not have happened. Maybe I wasn't paying attention to what I was doing as I was going down? Misjudged?" She looked perplexed and Alice could tell that she was hoping for some type of explanation. Alice could not offer her one and gritted her teeth, patting Miss Clara's arm to reassure her. "Well now, you are just going to have to be more careful going up and down those stairs!" she said, feeling certain that The Mentor was becoming more aggressive and looked down at the floor, thinking. A sinking feeling roiled around in her gut:

How do you get rid of someone who is unwanted if you don't know if they are a someone at all?

❧

Alice's days and nights began to blend as she started going through them both feeling like a shell, hollow and uncertain of herself. When she danced, it had no feeling. The freedom she once felt as she moved was diminished, each step empty for her where it had once been full of joy. She saw him at the club every night now. His tall form always leaning against the wall in the back, watching her. *What do you want?!* she wanted to shout at him as she pushed on through her routine. Everywhere she went she worried that The Mentor would be there watching. She could not shake that feeling of his presence in her life, and after the incident with Miss Clara, not knowing what he was and the unpredictability of what he —or it—was capable of. She was not the only one who did not seem to not be themselves. A pall hung over the entire house, with all three women seeming more diminished. They barely spoke at breakfast, or any other mealtime, any more. It was as if they had all retreated, the others not treading onto or into each other's own little worlds any more. As the days went on, they all seemed as if they were fading, becoming shadows of their former selves going through the motions of when they were whole.

As she got ready for work, Alice passed by the doorway to Bea's room and thought she'd stop, leaning on it. Her friend was quieter than normal, subdued even for her, sitting on the edge of the bed in her pale green satin slip and brown stockings. Clothes and shoes and books were strewn everywhere, her normal mess, but Bea just wasn't ... Bea. Like her, Bea looked tired. Almost haggard even, unusual for someone who so highly prided herself on her appearance. Alice came in, sat down on the bed next to her and looked at her more closely. "Are you okay? Feeling alright? Your eyes are a little bloodshot."

"I haven't been sleeping well," she said as her large brown eyes looked up at Alice slowly. She opened her mouth to say something and stopped. She was tapping her well-manicured nails on a book. *Clickety-click click, clickety-click click click.*

"Everything okay with Mr. Soon-to-be-Doctor Johnson?"

"He's fine and dandy. No complaints there."

She hugged her friend and held her hand for a moment. "Maybe you just need some rest or something?"

"Rest, yes. Good idea. Wish I could though. You were right, you know?"

"Hm? Right about what?"

Bea looked off towards the doorway as if watching something in the hallway. Alice followed her gaze and looked over that way too, not seeing anything. "Nothing," Bea said. "Nevermind." *Clickety-click click, clickety-click click click*, went her nails again.

"If you like, I can stop by the restaurant and let them know you're unwell?"

Bea nodded slowly as Alice hugged her again. Alice stood up to leave, looking at her friend with concern. "Feel better, hon. Let me know if you need anything."

"What I need is for ..." Bea started to say, but stopped herself, waving Alice off. "Go on now, before you're late. Don't give 'em a reason, you know?"

Clickety-click click, clickety-click click click.

THAT NIGHT ALICE DREAMED THAT SHE WAS WALKING THROUGH the halls of a large house or mansion filled with rich, dark woodwork. Although she wanted to touch it, everything had a touch of gray film upon it and was faded, as if no one had been there for decades. Dingy. Dank. She opened door after door entering room after room until she walked into one with large ceiling-to-floor windows with sheer white billowing curtains, a cold breeze blowing them inwards. A deep blue tufted velvet couch was in the middle of the room and she sat down upon it. She found herself entranced by the undulating curtains lifting and so softly falling, lifting and so softly falling again. The ones to her right blew towards her, but when they dropped back down, she gasped as they enveloped the form of a man.

The tall figure walked forward, the curtain slowly falling away as it came towards her. He was dapper in his shined shoes, dressed in a tailored dark pinstriped suit with a white silk square neatly tucked into the front pocket. As the curtain fell away from his face, it revealed desiccated brown-gray skin drawn back tightly like that of a corpse. He—no, *it*—ran a hand over its skull-like bald head as Alice's hand flew to her open mouth. There were only empty hollows where there should have been eyes. The Mentor. It *had* to be. *What IS this thing?* The figure moved languidly with an assured confidence, a swagger, its movements smooth and elegant as it went over to a gramophone on a small mahogany table. Its hand set the arm down onto the record with a flourish, the needle gliding along the grooves as it began to play the blues song that she had been hearing every night.

Thump thump thump.

Alice had never hated a song more.

She could not say anything as The Mentor came towards her, terrified to take her eyes off of it. Alice scrambled back across the length of the couch, her hands swinging at it wildly as it came closer. Suddenly, with great speed it was inches from her face, its drawn mouth curved into a sly smile showing very sharp, fanged teeth. She put her hands up before her and it snapped its teeth at them as if to take a bite of them before it laughed at her silent scream.

"I do not know who or what you are ... you can't do this!" she screamed at it.

Its smiling mouth now turned into a sneer as it put a knee on the sofa next to her, its body next to her and its face mere inches from hers. *Too close! Too close! My God!* Alice thought, recoiling in disgust even further into the velvet of the sofa. The voice was all too familiar now as it leaned over her menacingly, sidling up next to her ear.

"Me?" it said, laughing again. "I do as I like. I told *her* to pay attention too when I was in the hallway." It tilted its head, as she took a swing at it.

"Didn't you hear me?"

❧

Alice woke up sweating and still swinging at the air. The sense of dread did not leave her as she quickly got out of bed. She needed some water. Something, anything, to still herself and to help her try to forget that experience.

Then she heard it.

Thump thump thump. The bass. The tinny piano. The doleful singer. Coming from ... Bea's room?

She ran to the door and knocked. Nothing.

She banged on it. Still nothing. Normally, Bea would have answered by now, groggy and annoyed.

"What is going on?" Miss Clara said, limping out into the hallway in her robe, a scarf neatly tied around her hair.

"Something's wrong with Bea, Miss Clara!" Alice banged her fist against the door to no avail. As loud as she was being, there was no way Bea couldn't hear her.

"How do you know that? Maybe that girl is sleeping hard, so leave her alone," the older woman said with a shrug, clearly annoyed at being awakened at this time of night.

"Then how come I can't open this door? You *know* that's not like her at all," Alice shouted, pushing against her friend's bedroom door. "Bea! *Bea*! Let me in! *Please*!" Hearing no answer, Miss Clara's expression changed to one of panic as well and joined her, knocking on the door and calling out Bea's name.

Alice finally turned the knob, took a deep breath, and threw herself against it as hard as she could. It opened just enough for her to be able to get in. She wedged herself through the space in the door and grimaced as her bare feet stepped into something wet. *What in the world did Bea go and spill this time*, Alice thought as she made it all of the way into the room.

Like her own room, at night everything seemed an unusual combination of darkness, light, and shadows. Except for one. As her eyes scanned the room and readjusted, she jumped and let out a startled gasp as she saw a tall dark figure in the corner standing there watching, its hand held outwards, pointing. *Him.* Alice heard it laugh and it disappeared just as her eyes followed to where it was pointing. She then saw why the door had been so hard to open. Bea was lying on the floor in front of it covered in blood—her own. And Alice was standing in a pool of it. Bea hadn't just slashed her wrists —her forearms from her wrists to her elbows had been opened as if she had wanted to be certain. Her eyes, void of their soul, were rolled upwards staring, her mouth slack.

Then she heard it, that voice, whispering in her ear as if standing right next to her.

"Told you."

Alice started to scream and was still in that same spot screaming when help arrived.

WHEN HER FAMILY CAME TO COLLECT BEA'S THINGS, HER SISTER grabbed Alice's hand and pulled her aside as they were leaving out. "You were her best friend. Did you know anything? See anything wrong?" Bea's sister asked with a quavering voice filled with a desperate grief. Alice just shook her head from side to side over and over again, her own eyes beginning to fill with tears. "Alice, the police are trying to say she did it over her relationship and we all know it wasn't. Johnson's heartbroken. He was about to propose, you know. Had a ring and everything. We're all just trying to understand what happened here."

"I'm trying to understand too," Alice said, letting her hand go.

PAY ATTENTION...

It was all that Alice could do *not* to as she tried to go to sleep that night, but it was insistent. She could hear the music, *thump thump thump*, and the now familiar voice was right in her ear—that even, low, caressing baritone that was soothing, yet not, at the same time.

"I told you before and you did not listen. Look what happened. Will you listen to your mentor this time then?" it said.

Alice's eyes flew open as she sat up in her bed, looking around. All she could see was that faded gray-blackness of the quiet of night, shapes and shadows and forms whose meaning had to be discerned first before everything was comfortable again. She thought of Bea and a visceral anger, deep and resonant, welled up from inside of her. Hearing that voice did not scare her this time as so many times before. This time invoked unbridled fury. For Bea. For Miss Clara. For herself.

"You should've left her alone!" she shouted out into the dark-ness. "Go away! You are no mentor. You are not welcome! Leave *me* alone!"

"Aww, don't be like that. Why would I *ever* want to leave you alone? Don't you even want to know who I am?" it said with a voice as smooth and sweet as syrup. "You've been calling me "The Mentor" and *I* never said that was who I was."

I said to call me "Tormentor." Where you go, I will as well.

Alice's eyes widened at the realization.

See … you weren't paying attention at all.

A CLINK OF CRYSTAL GLASSES HEARD

Neeka was not quite sure how to feel about it.

Blood for blood, they kept telling her over and over again, and that was the extent of the knowledge that she had. There is something about how adults whisper things among themselves in hushed exchanges and furtive, darting glances and how they changed a conversation when one of them walked in. How they are such keepers of knowledge even as Neeka and her friends were becoming women just like them, despite protests that being like their mothers was something they definitely didn't want to happen. Why would she want to? She could be someone entirely different, better even. Isn't that the way of things? The way things are supposed to be?

Neeka still couldn't begin to fathom everything they might know though. There was so much excitement about who she and her friends were becoming, but it was the mystery of it that was so intriguing. The things that have not been, the things that are yet to come. She once tried to ask her mother about it and was told "You'll see when it happens to you." What kind of answer is that?

She had known her friends Zina and Laila her entire life. Their moms had been best friends for all of their lives and would get together and drink wine and laugh and talk as the girls hid out in each other's rooms and basements. This time they sat in Neeka's room and tried to piece together what little they knew as their mothers' raucous laughter floated up to them from downstairs.

"My mom always seems really different then, you know? Just not herself," Zina said, pushing back long purple-threaded braids as she stretched out on a thick, white faux fur rug. She pushed her glasses back up on her nose before spitting out a sunflower seed and pouring some more out into her hand.

"This might sound really weird, but mine just seems really ... hungry and sometimes she leaves out at night. I think she goes somewhere like a drive-thru or something since she's not hungry when she comes back." Laila pouted and then sighed. "I wish she'd at least bring me back a burger."

They all turned and looked at her.

"Actually, that sounds like mine," Neeka said.

"Mine too," Zina nodded, spitting out another seed.

"That's kinda weird though, huh?" Neeka said, reaching for the bowl of salt and vinegar potato chips. "I mean, is being super-hungry a *thing* then? I've never read anything online anywhere about that being a thing."

"Not that I know of, but then again, we only know as much as we know or they'll tell us, huh?"

"It kind of sucks that we don't know more actually."

Laila started messing with her hair, pulling it up into a bun with an elastic. "I wonder what they are talking about."

"Let's go listen in then," Neeka said and they slipped out of the room, crouched down and huddled at the top of the stairs. Neeka put a finger to her lips and the other girls nodded. That's when she heard her mother's voice.

"The girls are almost twelve. We need to go ahead and plan everything. The last thing that we need is for it to kick in and they are unprepared. If you're like me, this means your girls are pretty much in the dark about this too."

"Well, that is by design isn't it ladies?" the smooth, patrician accent of Laila's mom chimed in. Neeka had always found her a bit superficial and filled with airs that she chalked up to the upper-class world she was a part of. "I mean, after all, if they knew what they were in for ..."

"I just don't want to frighten them, that's all. I mean, look at us. We adjusted pretty well, like our mothers before us and before them." Zina's mother said.

"We'll have to give them some guidance, of course," Neeka's mother said. "We can't have them just going out in the world without knowing what to do."

The girls looked at one another. "I didn't realize that it was so serious like that," Neeka whispered. "After all, it's just our periods, not the end of the world right?" Laila shrugged as Zina grimaced. The voices downstairs got quiet for a moment and the girls snuck back to the room.

"Girls, come on down! We're leaving now!" the mothers called up.

"See you next month!" they said as everyone hugged and kissed one another. Neeka stood in the doorway with her mother, who had her arm around her as they waved.

"Next month will be special," her mother looked down and said to her with a smile. "You'll see."

⁂

THERE WAS SOMETHING ABOUT THE WAY MUSIC MADE NEEKA FEEL. Like reading, she often felt transported. Taken to a whole other place where she was somewhere else, maybe someone else. Untouchable even. Neeka's mother called upstairs to her and Neeka sat up, looking at the white Christmas lights she had strung along her dresser mirror. She had a collection of little cat figurines on it, something that started with one her grandma gave her as a little girl. She sighed as she responded to her mother's call, took out her earbuds and came down. "We are going out," her mother said, grabbing her purse and keys. "Now."

❧

HER MOTHER DIDN'T SAY MUCH DURING THE CAR RIDE AND looked over at her from time to time. The moon was full and bright that night, illuminating the night sky despite all of the streetlights. Neeka watched it and tried to keep it in her sight as the car made its way through the city streets.

"Where are we going?"

"To go be with the girls tonight."

Neeka's face scrunched up. "This is different. I didn't know we were all getting together tonight."

"Well, the last of you had your birthday, so we thought we'd get together."

Neeka didn't know what to think. They had both gone to Laila's birthday party. It was lavish and over the top like everything Laila's mother does and they had a great time together. Laila's family went all out for her. Neeka couldn't understand all of the fuss over a twelfth birthday. Sixteen, sure? It just seemed like a bit much. Her mother and sister took her out to eat and she was happy with that. This still seemed unusual though. She thought about how intently the mothers were watching them last month when they were there. She and the other girls had joked about it, dismissing their moms as "Weird like normal." No. Something else was going on. She just couldn't put her finger on it.

They were soon driving through what Neeka thought of as the rich part of town and pulled up in front of a gate. Laila's mansion. She looked over at her mother, who was looking straight ahead as the gates opened and they drove in.

She saw Zina's mother's car there too and started to really wonder what was going on. Laila's mother opened the front door, but she wasn't smiling like normal. She could see the other girls there looking just as bewildered as she felt and walked over to them.

"What is going on?" Laila whispered.

"Girl, we are at *your* house, remember? You tell us!" Zina said looking back at the mothers, who were starting to walk towards the kitchen.

"Do not go to your room this time. Go and sit in the dining room, please," Laila's mother called out to them. Neeka was disappointed, because she loved Laila's room. It was large and filled with what she thought was the best of everything decorations- and electronics-wise. She even had makeup! Although Laila had her moments, compared to her mother Neeka thought Laila was really sweet and just wanted to be liked.

The girls looked at one another again and went into the living room and sat down on one side of the mahogany table, with Neeka in the middle. For as many times as she had been to Laila's house, she never got over how sumptuous it was, like something out of a magazine. Her house was nothing to sneeze at and was nice enough, but this house was something entirely different. From the furniture to the artwork, it was an interior decorator's dream. The mothers came in one by one, each sitting across from their daughter. "We have something to tell you," Neeka's mother said. "And it is very, very important that you listen, as your lives will never be the same."

"Well, way to be dramatic Mom," Neeka said with a laugh, the other two girls joining in. They became quiet again pretty quickly when they realized their mothers were stone-faced in front of them.

"This is not a joke," Zina's mother said, using what they called her "professor's" voice. Many a university student had been given a lot to think about with it. Her long hennaed locs fell in front of her face. "Not at all."

Laila's mother then got up and came back with what looked like a vintage silver tray with carved crystal glasses on it. She set it down in the middle of the table and took one of the glasses herself, the other mothers following suit. "Go on," Neeka's mother said, pushing the tray closer to them.

"Oh wow," Zina said. "What's this about? Are you really letting us join your wine group?"

Once again, the mothers said nothing, their faces a mask. Each girl took a sip. They all looked up almost in unison and then at each other, confused.

Laila looked down at hers. "I ... I don't think this is wine. Mom?"

"You're right, honey. It is not."

"I feel kind of funny. Mama, what is going on?" Zina said.

Neeka felt warm inside, like her very veins were on fire. It was as if she was burning inside. She could swear that she could hear the heartbeats of everyone in the room. No, she was certain that she could hear every heartbeat at that table. *Loudly*. She looked across from her and her mother was watching. "Can you hear it too?" Neeka asked Laila and Zina.

"I think I can hear ... *everything*," Laila said. "Everything. Something is wrong. Why can I hear everything?"

"This isn't right," Zina said. "Ohh, this is *not* right."

"Yes, it is. Zina take off your glasses. You won't need them anymore," Zina's mother said as she reached out her hand for them. She did as she was told and had a shocked look.

"I have always worn glasses. Since I was little. What is *this*?" Zina reached her hand towards her mouth and opened it, touching fangs that had suddenly appeared. Laila saw her and screamed, her hands flying up to touch her own.

"What ... what is *happening* to us?!" Neeka said, doing the same after seeing Zina's. She started to panic.

"On a full moon of your twelfth year, we have to initiate you. It is as we have done. As our mothers and their mothers and their mothers did before them. We must share that generational knowledge with you. Tonight is that initiation."

"Blood for blood," all three mothers calmly said in unison, holding up and then taking long sips from their own glasses. "May the next generation be wiser than the one before and before."

"What is this? Some kind of cult? Or a sick joke, because this is sick! I do not want to be a part of this so you can count me out," Zina said as Laila started to wail.

"This is not. It is who you are. It is in your very DNA. You would not be able to help it and that can be dangerous," Neeka's mother explained.

"For who? Because this is seriously starting to feel a little child protective services right now, I'm just saying," Neeka said.

"You are a part of a long line of vampires. It only triggers for about a week once a month starting with the full moon. We're not like the Weres. You are not going to undergo a physical transformation beyond your fangs, and even those can be controlled. Heightened senses, heightened strength, and also ... a need for blood." All three girls' lips curled up and they looked down at their glasses.

"So, wait a minute," Laila said. "When you three were getting together for wine every month, that wasn't wine. It was ..."

"Blood, yes, darling" her mother said in that languid voice of hers, taking another sip and draining her glass.

"Blood, nooo ..." Neeka said in response. Laila leaned over from her chair and promptly threw up, the dark red vomit splattering against the expensive plush carpet. Zina looked ill.

"So, what now ... are we expected to go out and bite necks now? I am *not* biting people," Zina said, crossing her arms.

The mothers looked at one another.

"Oh God, no. That's what familiars are for. We have a network of healthy donor familiars. As long as you have a glass a day, you'll be fine."

"If not?" Zina demanded.

"Then your body can't function, pure and simple."

Laila started to cry. "I'm a freeeak ..."

"No, honey, just a vampire," Laila's mother said, reaching across and patting her hand.

Neeka's mother looked at each one of them. "These girls are now your Cohort. You will always be there for one another. They are your confidantes, the ones you should always be able to trust. Your own daughters, if you have them, will be like this as well as it passes without a doubt through one's maternal line."

"But really though. Can we control this? Cuz, I don't want to be biting people," Zina said. "Wait, can we turn other folks? Like in the movies?"

"No, this is genetic. You have to be born like this," Neeka's mother responded. "Trust me, there's a reason I became a scientist, and this is one thing I definitely know."

"OK then," Zina continued. "Soo ... are we immortal?"

All three mothers started laughing. "No, while you will live longer than most, you are not immortal. You can be killed and you can die. I swear you girls have been watching and reading myths."

"Well, it's not every day that myths become real, you know? Wait, did you say 'Weres' earlier?!" Neeka said, still struggling with the burning sensation inside that was now feeling like flowing ice water everywhere in her body. She just felt ill. The mothers shrugged.

Neeka felt Laila reach over and squeeze her hand. "I don't want to be a vampire!" Laila said, wailing. She seemed inconsolable. Neeka sat there quietly for a few moments before standing up. "I want to go home now. This just can't be happening. I want to go home."

The mothers sighed one by one. "Your grandmothers warned us that this might happen."

"Wait, Grandma is one?" Neeka asked.

"Yes, and your sister too."

Neeka sat back down and like the other two girls, was quiet. She hugged Laila, who wouldn't stop crying. Zina put her head in her arms on the table. Neeka just couldn't process everything that she was told tonight and what her future would be. A *vampire*? Just who in the world finds out of the blue that they are a vampire? Oh wait ...

Her.

***

THE RIDE BACK HOME WAS QUIET AND AS AWKWARD AS IT COULD be after finding out something like that. Laila was still wailing as they walked out of the door. Neeka kept looking over at her mother and finally asked "Have you ever fed on someone?" Her mother looked over at her.

"Well?"

Her mother turned back to the road. "Yes."

"Why? I thought you said you didn't do that?"

"Sometimes you are in situations where you don't have access to familiars or blood reserves." Neeka noticed her mother's grip on the steering wheel got a lot tighter. "And when you are really hungry, well ..."

Neeka was horrified.

"I'm sorry I asked now. I'd rather not think about it, if you don't mind." She started to wring her hands. Her mother's face softened.

"Baby, you have to and we will. I know that it is a lot to ask, but this will be as normal to you as breathing. You are not always going to be comfortable. There will be moments that you hate it, but it is part of who you are as a woman. You will come to see it, as we all have, as something that makes you truly special as one." She reached over and squeezed Neeka's arm gently. "You are part of a very long line with a history that I will continue to share with you and want you to be proud of. I just want you to feel empowered and unafraid as you go forward in the world now. Know that I love you. We all do."

They pulled up in front of the house. Her older sister Cynthia was home from college. She was standing in the doorway waiting, waving to them excitedly.

As they walked in, she took Neeka's hand before hugging them both. She looked at their mom and then smiled at Neeka before hugging her tightly.

"Welcome to the Sisterhood."

HERE, KITTY

Josie passed by the plain, pale-yellow house every day as she walked to and from her home to the bus stop. It didn't stand out that much and wasn't striking at all. There wasn't really a reason that it needed to be. It was just a two-story place with green shutters and a porch. Run of the mill. Average. Like most of the little houses in her neighborhood.

Sometimes its owner, an elderly woman named Mrs. Mills, would sit outside on her porch in a plastic chair, a slightly warped, cheap, white one with a leg that buckled as she shifted around in it. She seemed friendly enough and was one of those persons who liked to keep an eye on the community. Nothing missed her watchful gaze.

Ever present in her striped cotton housedress, knee-high stockings and black shoes, she would chide the kids and teens one moment, then ask them about school and tell them to "Do good!" the next. If she was out, she'd greet you as you passed. If the weather wasn't so great, she would sit in her front window instead. It was just what she did, and she had become a fixture, in a way, because of it.

One crisp, early autumn day, Josie was walking home from the bus stop, as usual. Her day at work had been long. *Anyone who thinks being an administrative assistant is easy is crazy*, she thought, shaking her head. Her phone started to ring, and she stopped on the sidewalk in front of Mrs. Mills house to dig through her large handbag to find it. By the time that she did, it had stopped ringing. She noted that the battery was almost dead, and sighed as she hoisted her bag back up onto her shoulder.

Just as she started to walk away, Josie heard the creak of a screen door opening, and Mrs. Mills leaned out, waving a dark brown hand at her.

"Hello! Hello there, young lady!" she called out.

"Hello!" Josie said with a wave back as she resumed her walk home.

"Wait, wait!" Mrs. Mills said, stepping out onto the porch. "Young lady, do you mind helping me out for a moment, please?"

Josie turned, facing the metal chain-link fence around the woman's small front yard. There were a few scraggly flower bushes in need of a trim, and a little statue tucked among them. *Probably a garden gnome or some knick-knack like that*, Josie thought as she came closer to the gate.

"How may I help you?" Josie asked with a smile. The older woman's face was elated.

"It is my cat, Kiki. I can't find her. She's here in the house, and I'm afraid that she might be stuck somewhere and can't get herself out. Can you help me find her?"

"I can try," Josie said as she made her way up the wooden steps onto the porch.

Mrs. Mills' warm brown eyes lit up. "Oh, thank you, young lady! Thank you so much! That is so kind of you. Come on in! What is your name dear?"

She smiled back as she stepped through the doorway into the house. "Josie, ma'am. I'm Josie."

Like its outside, the inside of the house was simple. Mrs. Mills led her to a small front living room. A slightly worn, dark red, tufted couch took up most of it, a multicolored crocheted afghan blanket carefully folded along its back. There was a wooden coffee table and end table. There were a few photos of Mrs. Mills when she was younger. Family members. Her with a man that Josie assumed was Mr. Mills. In one photo, they were dressed up for a fancy event of some sort.

"You can put your bags down in that chair over there," the older woman said as she pointed to one that matched the dark red fabric of the couch. As Josie walked over to it, she noticed that there were small cat figurines, all black. Some porcelain. Some wood. All different shapes and sizes and variations on the black cat theme. Mrs. Mills saw her looking at them.

"Kiki is black," she said wistfully as she lightly touched one of them. "So I buy ones that remind me of her. And sometimes people give 'em to me. Black cats are so sleek and mysterious. I love them. Don't you?"

"They are alright, I suppose." Josie said with a smile.

Mrs. Mills led her through a small dining room, its table set with china and a centerpiece, and they walked through an arched doorway to the kitchen. "May I offer you something? Make you some tea first? I find that tea really calms me."

"Oh no, ma'am. Don't go through any trouble for me, please."

"It really isn't any trouble at all, honey. It's the least that I could do for your helping me out." Mrs. Mills opened her refrigerator and pulled out a plastic bottle of water. "How about some water? Would you like that instead? I also have some juice ..."

Josie smiled. "Alright then. I would like some water, please." Mrs. Mills handed her the bottle and walked over to a cabinet to get her a glass. "Oh, no need," Josie said, holding up the bottle. "I'm fine with drinking it out of the bottle."

Mrs. Mills smiled and gestured for her to take a seat in one of the high-backed kitchen chairs. As Josie sat down, Mrs. Mills did as well, her hands folded in her lap. Her gray hair was well-coiffed in a roller set, not a curl out of place. She pushed her dark-rimmed glasses back up on her nose.

"I have lived here for a long time now," she said. "It has been quiet for some time now. The neighborhood has changed a lot. It used to be rougher. Really rough. A tough time for us all here who remembered when it was a good place. There were drug dealers and crack addicts and all of the drama that went along with that. I'm glad those times have ended here."

Josie nodded. "A lot of communities had that happen. Sadly, some still have it happening. It seems to be a nice neighborhood here now though. I like that it is quiet."

"Well, it's quiet because things got really cleaned up. Young people like you are moving here and making it different too. There used to be a whole lot of random deaths. Girl, there were just bodies turning up left and right. They said some of them were even mutilated. Some were just ... pieces left. Cops never figured out who was doing all of *that* kind of mess. Never found 'em and no one ever admitted to it. For all we know they're still out there, you know?"

Josie looked alarmed. "That's horrible! I am so glad that it's gotten better, that's for certain." She sipped from the bottle and finished the last of the water. She set the bottle down on the table.

"One thing about it being quiet is that it is definitely a lot harder to get away with things around here now. There are way more eyes. Way more persons paying attention to what's going on."

"I could see that." Josie said as she nodded again. Mrs. Mills smiled at her. "But given everything that had happened in the community, that's a good thing though, isn't it?"

"Oh, you have no idea."

Josie looked outside the kitchen window and frowned. "The sun is starting to go down, so I'd like to try and help you find her as soon as possible, in case I need to look outside, too." She stood up.

"I don't think that you will need to go outside. She's very much a house cat. I'd *never* let her out there. She wouldn't be out there. That would be a bad idea." She shook her head emphatically.

Josie shrugged. "Alright then. Let's go and find Kiki."

⁂

MRS. MILLS LED HER THROUGH THE HOUSE. THEY STARTED IN THE kitchen, looking everywhere. They opened the small pantry filled with canned goods and little containers, its single light bulb overhead. Josie opened wooden cabinets and peeked into boxes. She checked under the metal-legged table with its plastic tablecloth covered in a red rose design.

"Well, she is not in here," Mrs. Mills said as Josie closed the last of the bottom cabinet doors. Josie nodded in agreement. They checked the back room thoroughly. Nothing but a washer, dryer and utility sink. No Kiki. She shook her head. "No, not in here either."

They walked back towards the front door and stopped at the bottom of the stairs to the second floor. Josie waited patiently as Mrs. Mills took her time carefully going up the steps, sometimes pausing to catch her breath as she used her cane for leverage.

"*Ooof* ..." she grunted as she planted the cane down solidly on the step ahead. "My knees just ain't what they used to be, you know?"

"When was the last time you saw Kiki?" Josie asked as they slowly made their way upstairs.

"Hmm... last night? The last time that I saw her was last night. I think that she has to be really hungry by now." She steadied herself with the railing as she went up the last step. "I have to take care of her. She is really something special. She's all that I have left now."

There was a small bathroom at the top of the stairs. Josie took a peek inside, just to make sure Kiki wasn't napping in the tub or in the cabinet under the sink. No. She wasn't in any of those places either. She sighed a little bit. "Are you sure that there is not any way that she could've gotten outside?"

"Oh no. She really is an indoor cat now, remember? She's not allowed outdoors *at all*. Who knows what kind of trouble she would get into out there, you know? All sorts of bad things could happen."

They went into the smaller of the two bedrooms. It had a plain bed with a dark wooden headboard. The bed was neatly made up with a cream-colored bedspread. A braided rug was on the floor beneath. A wooden dresser was against one wall, a white lace doily spread across its top. There were framed pictures of beautiful geometric designs. *So pretty! How artsy of her*, Josie thought.

More black cat figurines were arranged on top of the dresser. *It's a bit much, but I guess she really, really loves this cat*, Josie thought to herself with a smile. *She does seem to have a touch of cat lady to her. Honestly, I'm surprised that she only has one of them.*

Mrs. Mills stood in the doorway watching as Josie lifted the bedspread and peeked under the bed, Then she opened a musty-smelling closet of old clothes. Her hand brushed against some dark velvet fabric with gold embroidery. A cape or cloak of some sort. *That must have been beautiful to wear out to somewhere nice*, Josie thought as she closed the door.

"Doesn't seem to be in here Mrs. Mills. This is crazy. I'm really wondering where she is."

"On to the next room then, Josie. I hope we find her. I hate to think that she could be stuck or something's wrong. I have to watch out for her. She can be a very tricky one to deal with sometimes."

Josie laughed. "Cats can certainly be like that."

"Do you have any pets?"

"No ma'am. Unfortunately, the place that I am renting doesn't let me have any pets. I had some dogs growing up, but no cats. They creeped my father out. He said he always hated the way they seemed to sneak up on you."

"My late husband was the same way as your father. He really did not like Kiki at all. Didn't understand why I kept her. Until his end, he absolutely detested her and wanted nothing to do with her. He even tried to get rid of her once ..." Her voice trailed off. "Well, how about you Miss Josie? Do you like cats?"

"I like them just fine as far as pets go, but have never had any myself."

"Oh, a shame. They are so special." Mrs. Mills said as they walked down the hall to the master bedroom.

Josie always found being in someone else's bedroom—particularly a stranger's—for the first time to be a weird feeling. Their most private place. It felt almost intrusive, but Mrs. Mills didn't seem to mind at all. She sat down on a wooden chair in the corner as Josie searched around under the bed and into the closet again. Like the second bedroom, the master bedroom had a frugal simplicity to it. A plain bedspread as well as a colorful quilt was upon the bed. A nightstand had a small clock and a container for her dental work to soak overnight. There was a photo of a younger Mrs. Mills with a group of women sitting next to the clock. They were all standing together with serious looks on their faces. Mrs. Mills noticed her eyeing it.

"Those were my ... sorority sisters."

"A sorority? Which one? Deltas? AKAs? Zetas? I was never in one. They seemed fun, but I wasn't much of a joiner."

Mrs. Mills laughed.

"Sorry," Josie said. "Were you all close?"

"Yes, indeed. We were quite close. I trusted all of them with my life. We had some interesting times together."

"Are you still friends with them?" Josie asked.

Mrs. Mills looked sad. "I am the last one left."

"Oh no. I am so sorry to hear that. That must have been really hard, to lose all of them like that."

Mrs. Mills shrugged. "We all got older. It happens. One by one, we pass away." She quickly changed the subject. "Do you have any family or friends in the area?"

"I moved here for work not too long ago. I have more acquaintances than friends right now, you know?" Mrs. Mills nodded in understanding. "My only best friend—we had been friends since we were very little—died in an accident about two months ago. I was an only child and both my parents are gone now too. So no, I don't really have anyone right now."

"Not even a handsome beau?" Mrs. Mills said with a wink, smiling at her. "Or a pretty lady?"

Josie laughed. "There's this one person that I really like, but it's not seri..." She started to say more and then suddenly clammed up. She laughed again. "I feel like I've been rambling. I seem to have a tendency to do that."

As she passed the photo again, Josie stopped to look at it a little more closely. They were all dressed in the same dark velvet robes, like the one she'd brushed up against. "You're dressed alike. I know how much sorority sisters like to wear matching things. Was this for a theme party or special occasion?"

Mrs. Mills looked at her and a strange expression crossed her face. "You could say that," she said as she waited in the doorway. Josie felt a chill, and quickly said "Well, she's not in here either. Is there somewhere else that we can look? I've got to get going soon."

Mrs. Mills sighed. "I have kept you for quite a while. It has been so nice having you help me out like this, dear heart. Well, I suppose we had better check the cellar."

Josie grimaced as Mrs. Mills walked ahead and started to make her way down the steps. She hated going down into cellars. They were always the stuff of horror movies and nightmares: dark, dusty, and filled with unused, unwanted, forgotten things.

Mrs. Mills opened the door and flipped a switch. The light bulb overhead came on with a buzzing sound and the cellar was exactly as she expected: a dark, dusty nightmare.

The wooden steps creaked and felt unsteady under their weight as they went down. "Kiki? Kiiii-kiiii? Are you down here?" Mrs. Mills called out. Josie held onto the railing for dear life going down. The last thing that she wanted to do was trip and fall.

Even with the lights on, the cellar seemed dark. *Ugh, I hate base-*

ments so much, Josie thought as she followed Mrs. Mills and the tap of her cane on the concrete floor. Light filtered in through a narrow, bar-covered window, yet it still seemed dim and gray. Old chairs were stacked up in a corner. There were stacks of books and papers everywhere. A workbench covered with jars was in another corner. *Who knows what is in those jars?* Josie thought, shaking her head as they wound their way through the cellar. It wasn't large, but the stacks and piles were like obstacles as they made their way through.

"You know, I would think that we would have heard her mewing or something before now though, especially if she was stuck."

Mrs. Mills stopped for a moment as if to think. "That is a very good point! I haven't heard her meow or anything since this morning, either. That is rather strange. That is also pretty worrying as well. I am definitely worried that something's happened to her now!"

A film of dust seemed to cover everything, making Josie sneeze loudly. She stopped for a moment. Thinking that she heard something in response to her sneeze. Josie looked around the piles and stacks as best as she could. "I think that could be her! Maybe she really is down here. I would not be surprised!"

Mrs. Mills exclaimed "That would be wonderful!" and began calling the cat's name too. Josie joined Mrs. Mills and called out to the cat as well. "Kiki! Kiki! C'mon out girl, c'mon!" she said, imploring it to come out of its hiding place to them.

After a few minutes of calling out to it to no avail, Josie turned to Mrs. Mills. "You know, I really could've sworn that I heard something move around down here. Maybe I didn't?"

"Well, let's keep looking then?" Mrs. Mills said, walking ahead until they reached a door towards the back of the cellar. It was locked. Josie stood and waited as Mrs. Mills unlocked it. The older woman pulled on the door latch and found it hard to open. "*Mmph!*" she grunted. "This door sticks a little. Could you give it a try?"

Josie shrugged and said "Sure, I'll try." She stepped forward and easily opened it. The room beyond was dark, so dark she couldn't quite see anything at all. She thought she saw movement on the far right of the room.

"Kiki?" she called out, thinking that the cat had somehow gotten herself locked up in there at some point. She heard shuffling sounds from the other end again. "C'mon girl. C'mon out."

In the dimness of the room, a dark shadow raised itself up at the other end in the direction from which she had seen the movement. *What the ...?!* she thought, her eyes becoming wide. *This can't be happening. What IS that??* Josie thought that her mind had to be playing tricks on her in the dark. Then, two very large yellow glowing eyes opened, looking directly at her in the darkness. This was no kitty. She didn't know what this thing was, but this was not a cat *at all*.

It was then let out a long, low growl. She screamed and jumped at the sound of it, everything in her knowing that she needed to leave. *Now.* She backed away from it towards the door, her eyes still on whatever that creature was that was in there with her.

It was then that Josie felt hands on her back, shoving her forward into the room with surprising force. She fell down onto her hands and knees, shocked and rattled as she scraped them against the hard ground.

She staggered to her feet, struggling to try to comprehend what had just happened to her. Then she heard the door quickly shut, and the click of its lock behind her.

Wait ... WHAT?!

Josie whirled around and started banging on the door with both fists over and over again, screaming in panic. "Mrs. Mills! Mrs. Mills! *Please!* What are you doing?! *What is going on?!* Let me out! Please! Oh my God, open up and *please* let me out!"

She kept banging on the door, and then the realization that it wasn't going to be opened truly sank in. Josie started to shriek as the beast advanced in the darkness, its glowing yellow eyes getting closer and closer.

She could hear Mrs. Mills' voice from the other side of the door.

"Oh honey ... thank you! You have found my Kiki! Now you know why I just couldn't possibly let her outdoors. Way more eyes now. So much trouble she could get into." She paused for a moment. Josie could hear Mrs. Mills' footsteps and voice getting fainter as she walked away.

"You really should've gone ahead and accepted some of my tea though, dear. It would've made everything hurt a lot, *lot* less."

HIDDEN

I did not land
So much as
I appeared.
I do not know
This place
I see.

In the darkness
There are lights
In this cavern
There is life.

I do not think
I should
Be found.

EMPTY VESSEL

St. Francisville, Louisiana: 1821

This is one of my favorite places. It's where I'd like to stay. Sometimes you'll find me walking along the long front porch, trailing my hand along the verandah's grillwork with its iron clusters of grapes and leaves. Often I wander in the gardens or watch folks coming in through the gates. This place suits me just fine.

I wonder where the children are, but I think they're scared of me. There are many others who live here too, but we are all preoccupied in our own worlds and playing an elaborate game of hide and seek.

There was no question that working in the house was easier than having to be out in those fields with its hard life of toil, sweat, and beatings. House life was better, but brought its own trouble. All I could comfort myself with sometimes was being able to get out of that sun.

My momma was a mulatto woman and they used to tell me I took after her with the dark, wavy hair and dusky-brown skin. After me, she became barren—a useless slave woman with an empty womb—so they sold her. They said her master was a Frenchman and my papa, but the only papa I knew was a strong field hand named Aaron that loved her. It was that very strength that made the owners keep him, and I could only hope it sustained him when I was sold away from him too.

I missed my papa's stories, his smell, and the way he hugged me with his laughter. In my dreams I saw his face.

I wondered if he could see mine.

❧

I was raised by Nana 'Tima, who told me about the villages and places where she had lived as a free young woman before she was caught and brought over on the ships. Her stories of her home where peach sands covered the ground and trees grew with trunks so wide people could live in them sounded like heaven on Earth.

She taught me about herbs and things that could heal or harm. "Don't go around here puttin' roots and goophers on folks," Nana 'Tima once told me as I went with her on her rounds.

"Yes, ma'am," I said, adjusting my white oak basket that was filled with little jars of poultices and salves and other things. How many times had I gone into the woods with her to help collect the ingredients?

"I am teaching you this to help and heal, not to do bad with it," she said. I paid close attention and soon was able to remove hexes, make mojos and protection talismans, and help heal sick folks. Everyone respected my knowledge and came to me often.

Years later, I held Nana 'Tima's hand as she passed on and as I looked into her eyes I felt so lost and alone in the world yet again. There had always a void in my very being, my deepest soul, which could never be comforted just by the thoughts and hopes of my parents somewhere thinking of me. With Nana 'Tima gone from me too, that hollow space only opened even wider.

How much more loss could I take and how much more pain did I need to reap before I fell into it?

⚜

MY DAYS WERE SPENT CLEANING AND COOKING AND LORD, THOSE folks had so many fine, fine things. For Christmas, Missus gave all us slaves presents, whether it was foodstuffs or for us house slaves, hand-me-down clothes from her and Judge. When Missus gave me mine, I just cried out at the sight of the satin dress. I had never owned anything so wonderful and its color reminded me of the green glass bottles on the tree near Nana 'Tima's. I held it against my skin and it felt so good I felt like a rich lady myself. I thanked her and she told me to try it on, since it was Christmas after all. I did as I was told and turned shyly in it for her. She told me how pretty it was on me and as I turned towards the doorway I noticed Judge staring. We caught eyes and he looked nervous and hurried away. I ain't think much of it. I took that beautiful dress and folded it up in my cabin.

Their things were so nice that sometimes I'd just run my hands over the fine linen or the shiny fabrics of the Missus' dresses and close my eyes. Liza, who was about the same age as me, sometimes did the same thing.

"Chloe," she'd say. "You cain't let 'em catch ya touchin' they things like that!"

"Liza," I'd say to her. "I ain't! You do it too! If they ain't caught us by now, they ain't gonna, so shush!"

Liza's tan face would frown up and she'd continue with her dusting, sweeping, folding or whatever task she had at the moment.

One of my favorite things to do was to watch over the children. I loved their bright little faces and small clothes. What a shame that the little ones like me couldn't have those nice clothes too. It just wasn't right. I would see the little slave children in their tattered rags and it tore at my heart.

JUDGE WAS KNOWN FOR BEING WITH THE LADIES—WHITE ONES like him or slave ones like me. Didn't matter to him, so I wasn't surprised when he started making eyes at me. One day he touched my hair and I jumped back when he did. I didn't know what to think, and was shocked the night he came to my cabin and asked me to put on that green dress.

What was I to do? I did what my massa told me to do. I put on that green dress.

When he took me to bed, I wasn't Chloe anymore. I wasn't anyone anymore. I was nothing but just maybe, just maybe, just <u>maybe</u> an empty vessel to be filled up so my life could be different.

WHEN HE WANTED ME, I WENT. WHEN HE SUMMONED ME, I followed. I realized I needed him if my life was going to stay the same. I couldn't go out in the fields! I've seen those scars from the lash of the whips! I've tended to those poor souls who got beat down by the overseers or Judge himself. Put my poultices on and fixed up brews to make 'em better. It just was not a future I wanted for myself. Over and over and over I went to him and each time, I prayed in my heart for his seed not to take root while a piece of me died inside with every caress. I cringed inside from his touch. His fingers on me, his being in me.

Then, one day, he didn't call for me. That day turned into many, and then the days into weeks. I was frantic with panic. He would look at me, then turn away. Was he sending me to the fields now that he didn't seem to want me any more? The very person I wanted to see the least I felt I needed to recognize me the most. I was devastated. Then obsessed.

"Chloe," Liza said to me one day. "You alright?"

"What do you mean?" I asked her.

"I know, Chloe," she said. "All of us know 'bout you and Judge. Even the Missus knows, but what can she do? Judge got the monies. It's a wonder she ain't done nothin' to ya herself. I've heard some stories about them gettin' payback on the slave womens they mens lay down with ..."

Her voice seemed to chatter on and on to me as she continued. I felt as if I was falling inside. She leaned over to pick up a basket. "Watch yo'self girl. Watch yo'self."

I sniffed at her. Watch *what*? What's to watch? *At least not anymore.* What had I *done*?

I started listening at doorways, stopping outside of rooms when I heard his voice. I wanted an inkling of news, something, *anything* to explain my rejection. To hear if I'd be sent out into the sun and headed for backbreaking work. I may have been a slave, but I was a woman first—I also needed to know why I wasn't wanted any more.

Turning to the children for diversion, I found they mostly happily played and laughed—oblivious to us slaves except to tell us what to do. It was truly their world and sometimes it was nice to escape within it. Often I played tea party and wood blocks with them, but inside me, there was this empty, gnawing, hurting ache in my soul at knowing that perhaps I'd failed.

Then one day, I'd gathered up some laundry and walked down the hallway. Passing Judge's room, I thought about being out in those fields. Hearing a noise, then his voice, I stopped and stood there quietly listening to what I realized were muffled moans and grunts. The noises stopped and I felt my face go hot from what I'd heard. Before I could recover, the door was snatched open and I was horrified to find myself staring straight into Judge's face. Liza was in the background hurriedly trying to get back into her clothes as I stood there frozen in terror.

He glowered at me, his face red, his mouth set, his eyes full of fury. No matter what I knew to do, I just couldn't move out of that spot. Where was I going to go? Nothing could help me. My mouth was open and a gurgled sound came out from my throat. Before I knew it, he struck me so hard across my face that I fell to the floor, stunned. He slapped me again in the face and I started screaming. My basket of clothing fell from my hands and rolled away from me —its contents spilled across the floor.

"You nigga bitch!" he yelled at me. I winced and cried and the tears flowed hot from my face. I was curled up in a ball with my skirts mussed about my legs as his blows flew furiously around me. Liza slipped from behind him with tears in her eyes and a stricken look on her face.

Liza?! Her too? Was she why he didn't want me anymore? How long? He had made her next! Oh no.

I didn't know if my next cry was from that knowledge or from the pain of his grabbing me by the arm and dragging me down the hall. My squirming and screaming only made Judge yank me harder.

"Stop this struggling or I *will* kill you! As it is now, I just intend on giving you and the others a little to think about instead," he snarled.

My eyes widened even more as I was dragged down the steps one by one and out the front door.

"Simeon," Judge said. "Go call the others to the front of the house." Simeon's kind, older face was confused and concerned, but out of his fear of Judge, he quickly headed down towards the quarters. It seemed like I was on that porch forever. Through my tears I saw groups of brown faces coming towards me. My face was stinging and starting to swell from the pain and my head hurt so badly from bumping it on the floor and the stairs that my ears were ringing.

"Get me some rope or twine," Judge said to Brooks, one of the overseers who accompanied the slaves up to the house. Brooks came back shortly and Judge tied my hands behind my back. I had stopped struggling and all I could do was lie there on that porch. One of the little girls started to come out of the house and she screamed, "Chloe! Chloe!"

"Take her back in!" Judge yelled to no one in particular. I saw out of the corner of my eyes that the someone who did was Liza. Her eyes were so sad and full of pity as she hushed the children and slowly closed the door behind them.

"Now," Massa said. "I'm gonna show you all what happens when one of you gets uppity enough to ever so much as *think* you have a right to listen in on my conversations or business."

Looking out into the crowd I saw young, old, short, and tall. All looked at me blankly, yet some did so with fear and others with anger. What surprised me is that I saw some looking on with expectation.

As I was watching them I didn't see Judge grab a long, sharp knife. "Help me hold her head Brooks!" he shouted. Everything happened so quickly that it didn't seem real at first. Brooks held my head and next thing I knew I felt an excruciating, searing pain as my ear fell beside me. Despite my howling and shrieking both from the pain and seeing my flesh lying on the porch stair next to me, I heard a collective gasp and felt warmth running down my head and neck. What was once my ear was now just a piece of me there— separate, separated. Judge said, "Let this be a lesson ..." and everything went black.

❧

WHEN I WOKE UP, I WAS IN SOMEONE'S CABIN LYING ON A cornhusk pallet, feverish and feeling as if I'd been blinded. There were shapes above me and a soothing voice I recognized as Auntie's.

My throat was dry and parched as visions ran in and out of my mind.

My father was standing there crying and getting farther and farther away from me and I could hear the creak of the wheels as the cart I was loaded into lumbered off down the dusty road. My cries were like echoes in my mind.

Nana 'Tima came to me, I know, and told me, "Hold on chile, hold on. Ev'rything'll be alright. It will ..." I saw her and wanted to be with her and I reached for her. As I did, my hand somehow brushed my head. Where my ear should've been was only a bandage of some sort now. I shrieked and flailed around until Auntie and another slave woman named Ona had to hold me down. Ona's dark chocolate skin gleamed in the heat of the cabin as she squeezed out a wet rag over a cracked bowl of water.

"Poor thing, poor thing," she muttered as she laid it across my forehead. She then prayed over me in some language I'd never heard before, but its tones were calming and melodic. I faded away.

I drifted in and out as I heard voices speaking. "That girl been showing off her fancy clothes hand-me-downs and look where it got her. Judge ain't want her and then went and did this to her!" a woman said.

"That's what happens when Massa Judge just takes a woman like that. Just wrong 'er and spit 'er out. 'member how he did that other girl?" a male voice said.

"Hmph," another female voice said. "Look who takin' care of 'er now. I'm sure Massa Judge don't think she so pretty now."

"Hush that talk," I heard Auntie say. "Hush that talk."

WHAT WAS ONCE MY EAR WAS NOW SCAR AND BUMPS—A HOLE that was just there. I didn't want people to look at it and see my shame—even though everyone knew, so what difference did it really make? It made one to me because I was a freak. A freak who was beautiful to no one anymore.

I went down to the water to wash myself once I was up again. Looking into the water I saw myself looking back and screamed and screamed, tearing at the image in the water until it dispersed and was at odd angles and curves—much like the real thing. I dropped to my knees as I cried and cried. I ran my fingers along the ridges of my former ear. I was disfigured. I was ugly. I was not me. I ran back to my cabin and went straight to that green satin dress. I ripped it up in a frenzy and tied the fabric around my head like a headdress. The most beautiful thing I've ever owned will now cover the ugliest.

I THINK THAT THEY CONSIDERED SENDING ME TO THE FIELDS, BUT the children wanted me near. Judge wasn't too keen on having me around, but the Missus seemed to take some sort of pleasure in seeing my misery. I was given more kitchen work and had to help Nellie the cook with preparing the meals. Cakes I made became a family favorite.

For lil' Miss' birthday, they asked me to make a cake. I went out into the woods and got some oleander and crushed 'em up real good and stirred them into the batter. I had such a smile on my face as I stirred and stirred. The pale batter folded over my spoon in thick, viscous swirls as my smile got even larger. This, I thought, would work.

THE OTHER SLAVES CAME AND DRAGGED ME OUT OF MY CABIN themselves upon hearing the news. The night was hot and muggy and I had been sleeping fitfully anyway since I knew the worst was coming. For hours and hours, I had been up there at the house trying to help. I never thought this would happen. When they came to me as a group, I went willingly. Once again, my hands were tied behind me, but this time by my own people.

"Those two chilluns and the Missus died afta eatin' your cake!" they cried. "We know you cooked it and we know you got the knowledge. We know what you did! We can't hide you down here no more or Massa Judge might come down real hard on *us* off of you! To save ourselves, we will have to take care of *you*."

I didn't struggle—just as always, it seemed. I felt so dazed and numb. I saw Auntie in the crowd with Ona and they were weeping. Originally, I just wanted to make the children sick a little so I could help nurse them back to health and be back in good graces. But the more I stirred that batter, the more I thought about how I was used —how he used my body. How I really *was* an empty vessel ... not to be filled up, but to be drained of my soul. Drained it right out of me along with my blood when he cut off my ear. I stirred myself revenge, which is sweet. So sweet, like an oleander cake.

THEY THREW ME IN THE RIVER AFTER THEY HANGED ME. THAT'S the snatches of the story I've heard folks say as I still roam these hallways, walk along that long front verandah, and wander in the gardens. Sometimes I have my candlestick with me as I look in on folk, hoping for a familiar face. All I see instead is their fear when they look at me, and once again, I am alone.

THIS PLACE IS A FAVORITE HAINT OF MINE, BUT IT'S WHERE I'D like to stay.

WHAT WAS THAT?!

You do not have to believe in ghosts, just in the possibility, and during my six years as a ghost hunter I had the chance to find out about that possibility for myself. Whenever I would share this, even those who were on the fence about their existence had a story for me. Over the years, I have collected them from family, co-workers, friends, friends of friends—anyone who had opened up to me about their experiences. My file is somewhat thick now. As writers, we often use personal experiences to inform our work and spur the imaginations of our readers and I am no different. In addition to the stories that I have heard from others, I can use my own.

Every city or town should have a paranormal investigation group or expert(s) and I spent much of my time as a ghost hunter with a great group that did investigations in D.C., Maryland and Virginia. We were often contacted by historical societies, historic sites and museums to come out and look into what was going on there. This was just before the proliferation of ghost hunting shows with their infrared cameras and other expensive (at the time) gadgets.

The very nature of ghosts is how common they seem to be. Over and over again, residents of homes or staff at sites with unusual things going on would tell us "We just wanted to know that we're not crazy ..." I knew from experience that they were not. Sometimes just our presence helped to bring them a peace of mind. I've seen and felt and been through some things myself. Like hearing quick, light footsteps going down the hallway in the middle of the night during a private residence investigation or the spirit who, when we listened to a playback, clearly told us "NO" when we asked if we were welcome there.

During an investigation at a Civil War field hospital, we were being shadowed by a radio show. One of their hosts, a tall, athletic guy filled with bravado, asked us what he could do. We all looked at each other and immediately said "Rookie duty." Our group had a method we used to break new members of their fear, usually done at a haunted former warehouse in Old Town Alexandria, Virginia. We told him to sit at the top of the stairs to the basement in the dark and just listen to see if he heard anything down there. All of us had done it ourselves at some point, so we wanted to see what would happen. We left him for fifteen minutes and continued our investigation. Before the fifteen minutes were even done, he came rushing up to us, trembling and shaken. When we asked him what happened, he said he could hear a little girl crying.

There were no children on site ... at all.

There were some real hacks and craptacular crackpots out there, trust me, but that's with anything. I think that with ghosts and ghost hunting, the very subject matter itself is so up for debate that it's like a field day on both sides sometimes. Of course, some would say the same thing about me for even venturing to say that "Yeah, this s—t is for real." All I know is what I've experienced first-hand. It's all that I can go by.

I once stayed at the John Brown House in Maryland, near Harper's Ferry. Everyone on site was downstairs excitedly talking when we heard heavy footsteps, like someone in boots, walking above our heads. Everyone went silent, slowly looking upwards in unison. As the floorboards were wide planks with spaces that we could see

through, we could also see that there was no one upstairs. I am
African American and so was a teammate, two of the very few ghost
hunters of color in the country. Over our monitors we could hear
the neighbors patrolling the perimeter and saying that they were
going to "get us." I realized that I was more afraid of humans than
of ghosts and was given a choice that night: stay outside in a tent in
the cold with the threat of the neighbors or be able to lock myself
inside the haunted house.

I chose the house.

My job in the group was as its historian and chief debunker.
Many times, the history would not match up to the stories at all,
making it easy to rule out. Other times? They were verified or
created more questions for us. And then there was Ireland.

Our group went to Ireland, investigating and staying at castles
and visiting historic sites such as the Neolithic cairns and tombs at
Loughcrew. The castles lived up to their reputations, including
Leap, a historian's dream. At one castle, a group of us went for a
walk to the nearby lake. It was eerily quiet as we walked through the
woods. "Oh no," Barry, our Irish guide said as he steered us around a
fairy ring, its white mushrooms creating its familiar shape. "Do *not*
step through that!" There were no birds singing. No animals were
stirring. Only silence and the sounds of the lake lapping against its
shore and the whistle of the wind. If there was ever a place that
could make you believe in legends, Ireland was it.

In the castles themselves, a housekeeper quit while we were
there after seeing "something" and our teammates heard voices and
saw a woman's ghost in an office. One castle particularly stood out:
Ross Castle in Co. Meath. A 16th c. tower stack with a great house
attached, I ended up copying its guest book, which was filled with
accounts through the years. We decided to investigate the top room
of the tower, rumored to be haunted by a pooka—a shapeshifting
entity. As we sat there in the complete darkness, the bathroom lit
up with a blue light and then the room itself would become even
darker. I could see shadows moving among us and just outside the

doorway. A clairvoyant teammate told us what was coming in and out, including one entity that was crawling, pulling itself along the floor. They also said that there was an older grandmother figure there who was keeping the spirits away from me. I have never run during an investigation, but I broke one of our own rules and literally *fled* down the spiral staircase afterwards. If there was ever a place where I could believe legends were real, it would be Ireland.

Many ghost groups don't last very long for the usual reasons such as time, egos, apathy, member attrition, boredom, burnout—and ours was no different, as we folded in 2007. It was a privilege to have had those experiences. After all, how many times do you get to have free rein at historic houses and sites? I use my experiences and those of others in my work, which tends to have elements of the supernatural or paranormal in them. For all that I know about ghosts, there is still so much to learn and maybe someday we'll have all of the answers. Until then, I will continue to share what I know with you through my fiction.

And who knows? Maybe someday you'll experience something yourself for real too.

VOX

Fallen among the stars
The light comes and I
Raise myself to it in welcome
A supplicant
My voice no longer my own.

I hear the howls of the Things-That-Are
Their maws snap and lunge
Vicious in anticipation
Looming near.

He steps forward, weapon drawn
I hold out my hand to him
To them
And they fall
From my whisper "Not now."

I kneel beside his body prone
Lifeless eyes
A fallen sword

Among silent beasts
I stand.

I have come to claim
My own
My self
Triumphant
Warriors
We are won

A PLACE CALLED HOME

ur world is dying. *Again.*

I CAN'T SLEEP JUST THINKING ABOUT IT. "DO YOU THINK THAT WE are going to have to leave?" I asked my older brother Rasheed, who was lying there in his bed looking up at the ceiling and obviously awake too. He might act tough and everything, but I could tell it was bothering him. "It has only been two years this time. We haven't been here long at all."

Rasheed groaned from across the room before answering. I was pretty sure that he was rolling his eyes too. "Look, Renzo, if that's the deal, then that's the deal. We've been through this before. The situation is not going to change and we're going to have to go," he said, sighing before turning over. "Try to get some sleep." He waved a hand in the air and the lights dimmed, then turned off.

"C'mon, Sheed. I feel like we just got used to being here. Like things were feeling normal. I don't want to have to go."

"Stop being a baby about it. We're going to have to go." He

turned over, obviously not wanting to talk anymore. He never wants to talk to me. I sighed and stared at the ceiling myself.

THE RUMOR HAD SPREAD THROUGHOUT OUR SETTLEMENT AND IT was all everyone could talk about. My best friends Tia and Levon sat with me at our favorite spot on a hill overlooking the town. We could see the mountains in the distance and the farmsteads on its border. Levon and his family lived on a small one just outside of the village where they grew crops and raised livestock. "I heard that this planet releases deadly spores every few years and another release is about to happen soon," Tia said. Her father was a scientist like mine.

"Well, I heard something about the inner core being unstable," I said as I laid back and looked at the sky.

"Really? I heard an asteroid was coming our way," Levon said. "Besides, our last planet had an unstable core. Could we really have that much bad luck to have a planet go out on us in the exact same way?"

"It doesn't matter. If there's something wrong, then we are going to have to go," Tia said, plucking a purple flower and tucking it into her braids. A small blue creature with large yellow eyes hopped excitedly beside her. She picked it up and put it in her lap, where it made itself comfortable as she stroked its long fur. Tia looked down as it made soft, cooing sounds. "I hope that I can take Lulu with us. Do you think that they will make me leave them behind? Can we even have pets while we are on the ship?"

"I don't remember," I said to her, trying to make her feel better. No need to upset her any more upset than she already was. "But I hope that you can!"

LATER THAT AFTERNOON, MY MOTHER AND I WERE SITTING IN the house when we heard the announcement. Her face changed, full of worry. "It's okay, Renzo, we have to go to the town meeting now. Your father will probably just meet us there." She called upstairs to Sheed, who came downstairs slowly. I think "annoyed" is his permanent mood now.

My mother took my hand as we made our way through the narrow streets. I didn't turn it down this time because I was really nervous. I don't know, holding it made me feel a little less worried. I didn't care what I looked like. Things must have been wrong because normally Sheed would tease me about it, but he didn't say a word. He was walking on the other side of her and although he was trying to hide it, I could tell that he was nervous too.

❧

ELDER LORRA HAD GATHERED US ALL IN THE MAIN SQUARE, HER gray locs in a headwrap of purple and orange patterned cloth that matched her robes. She was standing up on a high platform and our father was standing beside her with some of the other scientists. He could see Tia across the way with her family. She caught his eye and shrugged, shaking her head.

Elder Lorra raised her hands in the air, silencing the crowd. "I'll just get right to it: Our scientists have discovered an...anomaly," Elder Lorra said. Gasps and murmurs rippled through the crowd as she continued. "We are sorry to report this, but it has become unsafe for us to continue to inhabit this land. This...planet. What is about to happen is an extinction-level event. I know this is hard to hear, but we can't stay any longer and will need to evacuate immediately." Everyone turned to look at one another, those gasps now turning into cries and shouts.

"You said this would be the last time!" someone yelled.

"What are we going to do?" asked another.

Elder Lorra raised her hands again. "I know this is difficult.

There was no way that we could have known. When we got here there was no sign of any trouble. You know from living here that everything was working out fine." I felt my mother's grip tighten on my hand. I squeezed her hand back.

"How long do we have?" a voice shouted from the back.

Elder Lorra looked down for a moment before looking out at everyone. "A few days at most. As there is no true way to tell, we should leave as soon as possible. This is not something to take lightly and the last thing that I thought that I would have to say to all of you ever again. We must leave. We must go. Don't treat this lightly."

⁂

THE THREE OF US MET ON OUR HILL ONE LAST TIME AND SAT there quietly looking over the village. The blue grass seemed to shimmer as the breeze blew through their blades. The houses with their tan and white stucco walls seemed more quiet today, their residents moving in and out of them with purpose. We could see leaders helping to direct people towards the ships. Since the announcement was made, everyone had been nervous and scared. I was glad to be away for a moment.

"We're not going," Levon said quietly. Tia and I both turned to look at him. She looked as shocked as I'm sure I did.

"What do you mean you are not going?" Tia said, her lips starting to tremble. "But you have to. I—I don't understand."

"My dad doesn't want to go. He thinks it is a hoax and will take his chances because it might not happen," Levon said, looking down at the ground. "He said that a whole lot of hard work went into creating a home and farm here and making something of it. My mom has been begging and pleading with him to leave, but he's made his decision. He won't go and she doesn't want to go without him."

"But Levon ..." I start to say, but there wasn't really anything that I could say about that.

"I'm kinda really scared. If everyone goes, we're all alone and if this is real, then..." Tia leaned over and hugged him, tears starting to run down her face. I felt tears on my face too. I don't want him to stay. I don't want anything to happen to him.

"I'm sorry, Levon." I said, hugging him too.

❦

OUR PARENTS LED THE WAY AS WE WALKED THROUGH THE SHIP'S corridors. It felt so familiar. We spent so much time walking or running through them as we waited for somewhere to call home. The ship had been kept near the village with a crew that regularly maintained it. A lot of people had wondered why that was necessary. I guess we're all finding out that it was a good idea after all.

We stopped in front of a door with 5-14 in large type. Deck five. Apartment 14. Our apartment. Dad held his hand to it and the door slid open. "Here we are!" Mama said, trying to be cheerful with a large smile on her face as we stepped inside.

The air circulation systems had been turned on in advance, so it didn't have that musty smell that ship apartments get when they go unused for too long. "Yes," their father said with a groan. "Here we are again." Sheed took a look around, his lip curling up in disgust. "I can't believe that we are back on this ship," he muttered angrily. He still isn't really talking to me even though I've tried to. He hasn't really been talking to anyone. Black cargo bins with our things were stacked in the corner. They would stay strapped down until we were at our cruising speed. No need to unpack until then anyway so Mama calmly took her seat and began reading. Rasheed sat across from her, letting me have the seat with the view. Dad sat across from me and started talking to Mama, I could only hear pieces of what they were saying. Things like "They have a new prospective planet in mind, but it is a few light years away" and "They don't think we have to go into suspension. Well, at least not for the entire time."

The apartment lit up with a red light as the alarm started to sound. We looked at one another and leaned back in our seats, pulling our harnesses over ourselves and clicking them into place. Everything started to vibrate as we felt the engines rev up. "Here's to the next place we call home," their dad said, as the ship shuddered and started to lift. I looked out at the view and couldn't stop thinking about Levon as the ground beneath us got further and further away. The ship shook once more and within only a few seconds, we were speeding through space among the stars. I looked at my family for a moment before looking out at the blackness.

Here's to the next place we call home.

WITH THESE HANDS: A TALE OF UNCOMMON LABOUR

George Town, 1800

It is with a trembling hand that I write this. Given the color of my skin and the simple life that I have led and tried to create for myself so far, many would be surprised that I could write this at all. A breeze from the open window overlooking the river port makes me pull my woolen blanket closer about me. It is usually more normal than not for this swamp of a place to be humid during this time of year. I am relieved to have an unusually crisp early autumn night, but the chill I feel comes from another source.

The light of my candle is dimming, the tallow becoming low, but this must be recorded. There is an ivory trinket sitting here before me on the windowsill. It is precious to me. How it made its way to me is of no import, but the fact that it did at all is what drove me to tell this tale. I once bore arms in our war of independence and faced redcoats and fear itself, but this?

This is something else.

IT WAS THE YEAR 1796. I HEARD SOMEONE SINGING IN GAELIC IN the distance, their notes strong and clear and filled with longing. So many of those working here were from elsewhere, with homelands and families and loves either left behind or the reason behind such toil that they endured. So many sounds in the night. So many sounds in that place we were creating. European and Black craftsmen, artisans, and labourers, both free and bound, all had been working for years on a symbol of a new country—*our* country.

We still had much to do as we worked to build the president's mansion, or "palace," as some had taken to calling it. There were no buildings as tall around these parts, so the project loomed over us all, though we had not completed its construction. General Washington himself chose the site and even drove in the stakes with the Irish architect Hoban at his side. All around us, this new federal city was a collection of farms and rolling fields and still more infested marsh than town. When I would get the chance, I would take a moment from my bricklaying to sit up high on the unfinished second floor to enjoy the view of the Patowmack River as the sun began to set. The noise of the other workers—their shouts, exertions, and work-songs—ceased as I watched the colors settle on the shimmering water. Despite all the din around me, for a moment and only a moment—even if only in my mind—I was surrounded by quiet.

❧

"SIMEON, COME, YOU MUST JOIN US," EUGENE HOPE SAID, WAVING me over. His brother, Clifford, stood next to him and looked at me with a huge smile. Both were tall, their skin flushed deep golden-brown from working in the hot summer sun. Where Eugene was dark-haired and dark-eyed, Clifford was fair—his eyes gray and hair light. Both had easy laughs and I had worked with them almost since the cornerstone was laid in 1792. They had come with Williamson, the master stonemason who trained them as stonecutters. They had also worked at the quarry in Aquia, learning how to manipulate the sandstone blocks that would cover the bricks I was laying. Unlike I who chose this work, the brothers were on hire from their owner, a wealthy planter from across the river in Virginia, near the quarry. Some, the brothers included, said that this planter was also their father.

"When I am finally like Free Simeon here, I am travelling the world! I am going to hop on one of those ships like we see on that river over there and sail to places no one would even think are real," Clifford said, holding out an ale-filled tankard.

"We are going where there are beautiful ladies with silks and rubies," Eugene said with a grin, taking the tankard from his brother. "Hell, *we* can be covered with silks and rubies ourselves!"

"I have heard there are buildings, even larger than this palace we are building, that are encrusted with jewels and gold. I am going with my chisel and mallet ready!" Clifford said, passing the tankard to me. "What is next for you, Free Simeon?"

I thought for a moment as I took my sip. "Maybe I will meet a nice, good woman and settle down. Be happy with her. Have children. Live a decent life."

"Here we are talking about silks and exotic lands, and this man is talking about babies!" The brothers started laughing, but Clifford's face then became serious as he looked me square in the eyes.

"We cannot go on like this, Simmie. This building here means freedom, but I am not free. Neither is my brother. There must be a way to not be bound any longer. It is easy to think of children when you do not have to worry about them being enslaved," he said.

"Why you chose to come down here from Boston and Philadelphia, I do not know. Why bring yourself *closer* to all of this?" Eugene said with a wave of his hand. "At least away from here we could be our own persons so that when we finally settle down, our children can be their own persons too."

Two of the other labourers had been lingering nearby—a little too close, given the things Eugene and Clifford were saying. One spoke up and came over.

"You wish to be your own person? That can be arranged, my friend," he said, clapping his hand on Eugene's forearm congenially. The moment his hand touched Eugene's skin, the man's hazel eyes turned black. It was fleeting, but I am certain I saw it. How did no one else?

"Just talk, that is all. Only talk." Clifford said to them, understandably nervous. I realized that the second man looked exactly as the first—twins. Of a similar height, with those hazel eyes and dark, wavy hair. One nodded to the other and spoke to him, the language one I did not recognize.

"If you do change your minds, we will be at the small grog shop nearby," he said as they walked away. He clapped his hand on Clifford, who flinched slightly. I could not believe what I was seeing. It happened again. A touch and blackened eyes. How were the Hope brothers not seeing this too?

As we watched them leave, we all seemed a bit shaken. "That was rather odd, no? Where did they even come from?" Clifford said. "You do not think that they will say anything do you?"

"I somehow get the feeling that they will not," Eugene said, still watching them as they walked off to the opposite side of the work site. He groaned slightly, touching his hand to his head. "Does anyone else feel a little unbalanced? Perhaps it is the ale gone to my head."

"I feel a little off, too, brother," Clifford said. "This place and its heat!"

"Are you going to go and talk to them?" I asked.

They looked at one another, and then at me. "Of course! These liquor rations we get just will not do. We are only going to the tavern to refill our tankard. That is all." We all started laughing, but inside, I found no humor. Not due to what I heard, but what I saw, and what I saw? That, I could not explain.

❧

THE GROG SHOP WAS A PLAIN WOODEN BUILDING WITH ONE ROOM furnished with rough wooden chairs and tables. Eugene called out to a barmaid rushing by with mugs in her hands. The curls of her strawberry-blonde hair were barely contained under her cap. She stopped to look at him and rolled her eyes.

"The Hope Brothers. What are you two doing in here?" she said, handing her customers their drinks before coming back over to us.

"How's business, Mary?" Eugene said as she looked him up and down.

"As good as it will be," she huffed, pushing a stray curl back into her cap. "Now, Clifford, *you* can visit anytime. This brother of yours, though, well ..." Mary raised an eyebrow and pointed at Eugene with a smile before turning towards me. "And *you*."

Mary looked at me, her slate-blue eyes crinkling with laughter as I put my hands up in protest. "I do not know how these two have wronged you, but do not look at me! I am just here for the ale."

"Only teasing. As for that swill? You are more than welcome to it. Nothing personal, love," she said with a wink at the barkeep, her husband Sean. A burly man with a long scar on one cheek, he just laughed at her joke and shook his balding head.

The brothers looked around and saw the two men sitting in the rear of the tavern.

"Simmie," Eugene said. "We will be right back. We would just like to speak to them. Hear what they heard and what they are talking about."

Mary brought me my own mug and I stood, sipping, as I watched the conversation from afar. Once again, the men clapped the brothers on the forearm where their sleeves were not covering their skin. From where I was, I could not see if their eyes had that same strange effect. I continued to drink, still watching them, and soon, all four got up and walked towards me. I started to go towards them as well, having already paid, but Eugene put his hand up and looked at me with a smile. Clifford was smiling at me too. "Take care. Watch yourself," he said, nodding towards me. I assumed he meant my ale and the speed with which I was consuming it.

"I have drink," I said. "I am fine!"

One of the men looked at me and asked "Friend, are you sure?" I raised an eyebrow, held up my mug, and waved them off, watching them walk out of the door.

THE FOLLOWING MORNING, I AWOKE WITH A START, SURPRISED TO have slept in a bit longer. Normally, the brothers awoke earlier than everyone else and enjoyed forcing me to be awake with them. I got myself together and walked over to the small wooden building the brothers shared with some of the other workers. "Good morning! This toil is not going to do itself!" I said, using their customary wake-up greeting. Clifford came out first, after shaking his brother. They looked at me blankly for a moment, and then laughed.

"We must have had too much yesterday!" Eugene said as Clifford nodded.

"Too much? Is there such a thing?" Clifford said, laughing.

We walked away from the rough shelters toward our work areas. My day would be a hot one, spent at the brick kilns, and the brothers would be needed to help cut stone for the Scottish stone-masons and their apprentices. As they parted from me, I overheard one of them say to the other, "So much stone to cut. And Fitzgerald is worse than Imhotep himself. Do you remember when ..." and then their conversation trailed off.

Im-ho-tep?

Away from the gregarious brothers, I had a moment to think about their question regarding my future. Being free, I had a small place where I had been living in George Town, but staying there would have made me expend quite a bit of time travelling to work in Washington City. It became more convenient to live close to the project with the other workers. My parents had seen to it that I had some measure of education and apprenticeship. I had been trained as a bricklayer and thought my skills would serve me well. But then the War happened, and I ended up living in Philadelphia. I had not given that much time to thinking about what was next for me.

Perhaps I should have.

THE YEAR WAS 1799. I WAS HAPPY TO BE WORKING ON THE second floor. So much progress had been made. It would not be much longer until the stonework laid over the brick was completed. They were already debating the lime whitewash to be put over that as well. Work had begun on the roof and the exterior would be finished. As I worked high on the second floor, I looked out over the work site area. In the north clearing before me I could see the brick houses Hoban had built for himself and his assistants and the simpler wooden ones for the rest of us. I smiled as I took pride in hoping that someday when I was long gone, this structure I helped erect would remain.

There were many other things that I could have been doing, but for that moment, watching the Patowmack sparkle behind me as I worked was enough.

I was broken from my thoughts by Jack Smith, one of our foremen, calling up to me. I had another task to do and another labourer took my place as I made my way to the scaffolding. As I did, he began to scold one of the sawyers—a German fellow—for a minor mishap. You could see on the man's face how diminished he felt as the foreman's voice became louder.

I saw Eugene nearby as he came close to Smith. He acted as if he was clumsy and stumbled against the man, grabbing hard onto his arm as he did so. He held Smith's arm tightly there for a moment, and then righted himself. I could hear him apologizing profusely and I expected to hear the foreman scold him as well.

It never happened.

I saw Smith put a hand to his head and mumble, his words muddled and confused. He leaned against a stack of bricks for a moment before excusing himself and quickly walking away. I did not understand what I was seeing. The man below who was being scolded had been watching it all with a look of confusion as well. He looked up, saw me looking on, and hurriedly rushed away.

The next day, Smith did not show up to his post at work, having said that he was too ill to be productive. It was suggested that he have some rest, as he complained of feeling depleted and lacking entirely of vitality.

I did not mention what I saw.

MONTHS LATER, THE BUILDING WAS NOW A GLEAMING WHITE. WE had been celebrating the exterior's completion with extra whiskey rations after a dinner of salt meat, bread, and tea from the camboose. I took a moment to sit by Eugene and finally got up the nerve to ask him what had happened. Especially given that he had taken quite a chance with what he had done. "I must ask you. The other month ... with the foreman. What was that all about? That does not seem like you to interfere with someone else's reprimand."

I saw him shoot a look at Clifford before he answered and said, "This is not the first time. I have done it so many times, for so many others before."

By night's end, we had all consumed a lot, which made for loose tongues. So much so that even Eugene and Clifford's Virginia accents seemed to slip a bit. We told one another raucous stories, each one more outrageous than the next. But that night, the brothers told fantastical stories of incredible columned temples and pyramids with steps, grand libraries, and other ancient places of wood, of stone, of earth. Of palaces and fortresses, humble huts and gleaming, gilded domes. Of master builders and masons and soaring cathedrals.

"Realities can be both destroyed and made. We build because we can, and because it is what we have always done," Eugene said dramatically, holding his hands out with his palms up as we all cheered. "It is with these hands that we can create a new world such as this."

I wanted to blame it on the drink. I wanted to take it as more of their imaginings. Their dreams of a future denied. They asked me more about myself and the family of which I was now the only member. The places I had seen in my own travels that had led me to this point. I could not remember ever having a conversation of such depth with them before. Clifford watched me intently. "Simeon, are you sure you do not wish to see more yourself? You must want to be more than this."

"I am content with the life I have for myself right now, but only for right now. Perhaps I will return to Philadelphia," I said to him. "Although there is work here, I constantly find myself increasingly unnerved by the state of my enslaved brethren."

"As am I," he said. There was none of the strong sentiment of previous conversations as he said this, but in its simplicity, I was reminded of my own fortune and status. He looked at me again. "There are many who would give anything—including themselves— for a chance to be free, Simmie."

⁂

Our work on the exterior was done and much fuss was made when the Hope brothers disappeared. Their master would not be happy to have lost both the wages he made from them, as well as the skilled labour and training. There was much speculation as to how and when they slipped away, but I finally knew all was not as it seemed.

Just before they left, I received a package. Upon opening it, I found an exotic trinket that was surely from a land filled with rubies and silks: a small statuette of a seated four-armed elephant with one tusk and a large belly. I peered more closely at it and saw that its hands held different items: a bowl, a noose, an axe, and its own broken tusk. Upon the underside of its base the initials "E & C H" had been roughly carved.

It was then that I was certain.

I remember how the two men smiled as they saw me with it, my face dumbstruck as I turned the bauble over and over again in my hands, staring at the inscription. I still do not know how it made its way to me, but it did. My voice quavered a bit as I whispered to them "What...what *are* you?"

A question they would not answer, saying that they had no answer.

To this day, even as I sit writing this account, I shall never forget the simple statement I was told when I asked my other question: "Why?"

"For freedom, we took their place."

RULE OF THIRDS

Deep, dark, and far underground are the world's mysteries that remain, and I have been trying to discover them for my entire life. I stand here knowing that I am about to leave everything and everyone on land behind. As I slip into the warmth of the water, it surrounds me. Every time it is an embrace, a homecoming. One that even a hooded wetsuit or equipment or tanks does not distance me from. It is the unexpected that calls me. The thrill and sense of impending discovery and wonder that draws me back over and over and over again.

I see the rest of my team of three, Tim and the new guy, who are bobbing in the water, watching me expectantly as I check my instruments one last time. We signal to one another to begin our descent. I look up at the blue of the sky with its white clouds and then dip below. My team, like me, is here because of the lure and excitement of the unknown. One of them is new, which is why I chose to bring up the rear this time and put him in the middle. Everything about this dive has been planned to the abilities of the least experienced member. It has to be. In this case, it is our new guy.

We all laughed when we found out his last name is Karst, like the type of cave systems we often explore. "You were meant to do this," we said, teasing him.

I know that I was meant to do this too.

It is true that I never imagined this *could* be my life while growing up in our D.C. rowhouse. Brown girls like me were thought to be worried about messing up their hair, but I was always the first in the pool. I guess I was a little different? And I wanted something different too. I was a quiet kid who pored through all the books I could get my hands on about the underground world. I didn't fit in well with the other kids; I was told I talked about rocks too much. My mother indulged my passions, gamely taking me to cave attractions when we traveled, and she gave me an allowance that usually went towards increasing my rock collection. When I discovered there were scientists who explored underwater caves, I knew that speleology was what I wanted to do.

I can hear my mother's voice in the back of my head, saying, "Maileen, you don't have any business being under the Earth! And underwater at that?!"

I bristled when she called me "crazy" yet again before I left for this latest diving expedition, a deeper one than normal. I thought she understood, but I realized that, even after all of this time, maybe she didn't know me as well as I thought.

"I am a scientist, Mama. I need to know. We *all* need to know what is down there."

Her mouth twisted as she looked at me with sad, fear-filled eyes. "But why, baby, why do *you* have to be that scientist?"

⚜

IF ONLY SHE COULD SEE WHAT I SEE: THE BEAUTY OF GEOLOGY. These ancient places only a few—or no—humans have ever seen. Forests of delicate stalactites and stalagmites. Limestone formations like something out of a sculptor's imagination. Ones like bells. Others like frozen curtains of flowstone waterfalls. Shafts with walls that remind me of chipped arrowheads. Cream and rust colors abound. Water so pure that it changes from crystal clear as the air itself to teals and midnight blues. I love these places with their recesses and nooks and their isolation. Of being beyond everything. There is a stillness that I move through. There is also a stillness of my mind in these places that are so otherworldly and alien although we have not left Earth at all.

❧

OUR DESCENT IS QUICK. THE ENTRANCE IS STILL FILTERING LIGHT above us, but we will be going beyond the cavern into the depths of the cave itself. I have done this hundreds of times, but I have never dismissed my mother's concerns. All explorers face naysayers at some point in their lives, but this? Arrogance and mistakes down here can mean certain death. Perhaps from nitrogen narcosis. Perhaps from simply running out of air. Blacking out first almost seems merciful before drowning. I know the risks. All of us know the risks. But the risks are outweighed by one simple driving force: curiosity.

❧

THE PASSAGE HAS BECOME NARROW AND LOW. I AM AWARE OF SO much stone. The whole of the Earth is above me. It will not bear down or press upon me. This stone will not crush me. I can truly just let the weight of the world be as I calmly frog kick and glide ahead.

I am just passing through.

The idea of being beneath and within the earth, like a child in its mother's womb, never bothered me. You are ensconced and enveloped within stone and water, and there is absolutely nowhere to go but back the way you came, which can be a kilometer away. And if you are claustrophobic? This isn't for you. Some people like to jump off of bridges and out of planes. I like the quiet order of it all. Or at least the order that it forces me to have.

We ease ourselves forward carefully.

Control.

Control.

So much of doing this is about control. How important it is to be horizontal. How to make sure you can touch and follow your guideline. How to kick and move. How to not destroy those delicate mineral formations as you move through and around them. How to check your emotions and remain calm. How to manage decompression and especially your air. We have a rule of thirds as a bare minimum: enough to go down, enough to get back, and enough to have emergency reserves. You need enough to get in and get out.

Air is life.

❧

TIM TOOK THE LEAD THIS DIVE. A JOKESTER WITH AN UNRULY shock of graying hair, he is serious underwater and has done more cave dives than I can count. I know and trust him.

My mentor Rick trusted him. "Maileen, he's as good as they get," he once told me. "You know, besides *me*."

I miss Rick. I miss his gutbuster of a laugh. I miss his dry wit. His sharp mind. I miss him so much. One time he went down.

And then he didn't come up.

❧

THE WATER IS SO CLEAR THAT WE CAN EASILY SEE AHEAD OF US with our lights. We have made it through the narrow passage and there are junctions that branch off to other ones. Karst makes a stifled noise and shifts over as if startled, his tanks knocking into the stone and fins hitting the bottom. He swings his arms wildly in front of him.

What is going ON?

He moves erratically again, backing up towards me with his fins stirring up the sediment even more. I can't move backwards, but in the commotion I move sideways, my fins scraping along the bottom too.

No, no, NO! What is he DOING?! He needs to calm the hell down!

Wait ... Where is the guideline? I ... I can't find it. I don't feel it. That damn Karst has caused a silt out! My visibility is zero. I stop and swim upwards, but the water's no clearer. I cover my light against my chest but I can't see theirs. *Control. Control.* There's no need for me to panic. I've done the drills. I know what I'm doing. I've been through silt outs before. Yes. They would have put it towards the ceiling or near the floor. It must be here. I just need to feel for the guideline and follow it. It shouldn't be more than an arm's length away. Maybe it is along the wall? I reach out and there is nothing.

Nothing.

Oh.

Oh no.

I tie off my safety reel to the bottom and swim forward a bit more.

Nothing.

I stop and gather my composure. I've got to get it together. Stressing will just make things worse. I don't want to use more air than I should. Down here, survival is measured in breaths. I need to think.

Control.

Control.

I check my gauges. Still good for the moment. My equipment still works. My air is still good. Wait, one of my three lights has gone out. *Seriously?* It must've gotten damaged somehow. But it's all right. I have two others. I have two others and my air is good.

Control.

I reach out again for a guideline.

Nothing.
I swim forward again.
No one.
Oh.

❧

THERE IS NO CALLING OUT TO THE REST OF MY TEAM. THEY WILL tie off feeder lines and go back and forth along the guideline to try to find me, but that jeopardizes them as well once their gas supply dwindles. I know they will eventually have to call this dive and resurface. There were so many passages at that junction crossing. There is no telling how much farther I could have gone into any one of them. All of my training ...

Fucking Karst!

Lines from Coleridge's *Kublai Khan* come to mind to calm me: "Where Alph, the sacred river ran/Through caverns measureless to man/Down to a sunless sea." Maybe I will come out of this in Xanadu and discover paradise itself.

Control.

I swim forward again.

I reach out.

Nothing.

Goddamn you, Karst!

I stop. I reach out for the guideline.

Nothing. *Control.*

We are losing time. I am losing time. I am losing air. I am lost.

Control.

I reach out for the guideline again. This time someone takes my gloved hand and tugs, urging me along. *Yes!* They did not leave me! I'm going to get out of here. I'm going to be all right! Everything is going to be okay. I'm going to be okay. I turn to look at Tim or Karst, signal thanks, anything, as I am so glad to see them. Yes, even Karst. As one of my lights twists around in the darkness, I scramble backwards. I don't know *what* this is, but it isn't either one of them!

Oh God ... Is this what Karst saw earlier?! Is this why he was behaving like that?! What if there are more? Don't panic, DON'T panic.

Control. Control.

The creature is about four feet long and the size of a child, with thin, translucent skin. I can see its veins and even the outlines of its organs just beneath. There's nothing where its eyes should be, just recesses suggesting ones were there long ago. They are unnecessary down here anyway. What must have been its legs are now fused into what looks like an undulating tail. Gills flutter at the sides of its head, and feathery feelers protrude from what would have been ears.

I don't know its intent, but I just don't have the luxury of being panic-filled right now. What if it is a scavenger? What if it wants to eat me? But no, if it had wanted to do that, it could have attacked me before.

Down here, there are certain truths. Nothing about this is suitable for humans. We are so vulnerable. Normally I find comfort here, but I know that this is not our element and there is no comfort to be had right now.

Okay, okay. If we were attacked by something, there would have been nothing we could have done. So there it is. My decision is rational under the circumstances, as I have nothing more that I could possibly lose at this point: The only thing that I can do now is trust the creature.

It tugs on me gently, encouraging me to follow.

I do. Time is running out. I pause, then reach out. Its short arm is slim and, as I take its paddle-like, webbed hand I can only marvel at how the creature is not as fragile as I thought. In all of my dives, I've never encountered something so truly amazing. I wanted to find an untouched place, and a new species has found me instead.

The creature is quick and moves with certainty through the passageways. I can't take my eyes off of it, not just because it is my guide but because I realize it is as unknown as everything around me. It is, in a word: *wondrous*. Sometimes it stops and circles me, graceful as it effortlessly navigates the passage formations. We pass one I noted earlier in our dive, limestone flowstone like yards of supple fabric wrapped over and upon itself, pooling upon the bottom.

We ... are going back! It is taking me back out to the cavern! I look and feel around, and that's when I find it: the guideline. My team left it in place in case I was somehow able to find my way out. I almost want to laugh but find myself just shaking my head instead.

The creature releases my hand and goes ahead of me when we reach the low, narrow passageway. I take the guideline, just in case, as we make our way through. The creature slows down, pausing just ahead of me until I catch up. It goes forward. I catch up. Forward. I catch up. But it is never out of my sight. It never leaves me behind. Sometimes it makes burbling chirps at me that are almost startling in the silence. I want to smile, I am so honestly happy to hear it. To see it. I thought that I was glad for isolation and took solace in it, but right now I could not be more happy to not be alone.

I check my gauges and motion for it to stop. If we are really heading back, then I need to start to decompress as I ascend. Getting the bends would be painful, if not deadly. It makes a noise again, the loud echolocation sharp and clear in the water. It is amazing to me that, even in my fear, I can't stop thinking about how I have found something new. Something that I cannot even *begin* to explain, but I want to try.

The creature swims up close to me and chirps again, its hands patting me, touching my head. It is really curious, touching me with its feelers and short fingers. I allow it to continue to outline the contours of my mask, my face, but gently steer its hands away from my many valves and gauges. It burbles as it touches me, and there is a part of me that feels *honored* to have made this first contact. I can't stop looking at the creature. The way its gill stalks flutter. How it moves. That it even exists at all. It's so incredible, so unbelievable and beyond my dreams of what I hoped would happen down here. I am enraptured but need to draw my attention away, if only for a moment. I look at my gauge and signal I am ready by swimming ahead a bit, and it darts forward, reaching out for me.

I take its hand.

❧

WE COME THROUGH ANOTHER PASSAGE AND IT FEELS AS IF THE space around me has become more expansive, more open. Although still surrounded by stone, I know this means that we are now in the initial cavern. I can see trickles of light above me. My air is running low, but I know that I just might make it.

I will make it.

I look at my guide and it chirps to me again, swimming around and around me, refusing to go any farther. It must not be able to. I realize it has reached its own physical limits, a mirror of my own. My body cannot handle too much pressure. Its body cannot handle the lack of it. I understand and reach out for it once more. I take its hand and hold it in both of mine. I don't know if it would respond well to a hug, so I stroke it along its back like I would my cat, surprised at how much it feels like that of a salamander or axolotl.

Far above me, I can see the backlit shadows of my colleagues hovering at the surface in the final stages of their own decompression. I know that they are concerned and worried. I grab the reserve tank they left at the cavern's edge for me, just in case. There is something to be said about that kind of hope. That even scientists —maybe especially scientists—who know the odds still have faith in possibilities.

I don't know how to explain what happened but, now that I am out of harm's way, I don't know whether to laugh or cry. Why me? Why did it do this? Why did it choose *me?* All I know is that I owe my life to a creature no one in the world has ever seen before, and no one in the world may ever see again.

I reach out and hold the creature's hand again, giving it a light squeeze before letting go. I don't really want it to leave. I wish the others could see this too, but I know it can't be with me much longer. It is hesitant to leave, giving me another chirp. Then it zips away, its pale body a blur as it recedes into the darkness below.

This time I went down.

I am going back up.

PEREGRINATION

(CO-WRITTEN WITH CHESYA BURKE)

1919

H e breathes the city.

❧

NOT THE WAY THAT MOST PEOPLE INHALE AND EXHALE ON FUMES and the smog and the smoke of the industrial factories and labor shops on every corner in that god-forsaken place. But the way that one normally takes in oxygen to survive: he lives it, craves it, needs it. Sometimes, like now, he stands on the rooftop of the building, looking out onto the city, chest moving in and out with the rhythm of the night breeze, the birds chirping to the pulse of the moon. The moon has a pulse, if you haven't noticed. It swells and flexes in synchrony with the waves of the world. It breathes to survive and gives life to the Earth which in turn supplies the cities with life. And this, my friends, is how our small part of the universe works. The moon affects the waves, the waves affect the cities, the cities affect the people and the people make up the city. For always and forever.

What then of my little city breather?

The little boy who came out of my womb not screaming, but inhaling, seemingly intoxicated on polluted oxygen of urban decay. The son that I bore who quickly outgrew the teaching of his mother. The child that I do not understand anymore, one who speaks in riddles and takes breaths not of air, but of city itself. The one who lives and loves Harlem as if it gave him—and not me, his mother—life.

"They say the wounds of old men heal only when the heart breathes."

See, what kinda nine-year-old talks like this? "What was that baby?"

The moon foreshadowed him now and he was like a tiny speck in its glow. But somehow that was not completely the case, I knew. No, my child was not simply a speck in the shadow of this giant orb of light; he was an important part of it, he was a part of the whole city. I knew that as I breathed. And although I knew so little of the workings of the world, this was one thing that I did not question.

Harlem, New York—this city—belonged to my child.

"It's restless. Can you hear it momma? It needs more. But we cannot give it what it needs anymore." He turned to look at me, his eyes wide, wondering. "Can you hear it? It calls your name sometimes."

"No. I can't."

"Listen. Listen, shhhhh. It wants ..."

"Go on, what does it want, boy?"

The voice came from behind me, deep and wrong. I spun around to look, but I didn't need to. I knew who it was. His voice and the sly movements of his shadow on the rooftop floor would have given him away instantly. Looking at him now, I wondered how I could ever have been so fooled by this man, or whatever it called itself now. Whatever that was, I had no desire to call him anything. I had once known this being as Jacob LeRoy, a man who could move the winds and shadows without the benefit of the sun or moon or air; a man I admired and grew to love more than I even loved myself. But now I knew the truth. He was just as dark and uncontrollable as any shadow he manipulated, contorted, and corrupted into something unrecognizable and wrong. Just like he was. I instinctively moved toward my son.

"Go on now, son," he said with a voice butter-smooth. "Tell us. What does it want?"

"*My* son will not speak to you." Even so, I held the boy tighter than I should have, giving him less freedom than I pretended he had. It wasn't until I had time to think about it later that I realized that I'd belied my own words by practically screaming "my," as if I was trying to will away the other part of him. But we all three knew the truth, and only I was too stupid at the time not to admit it.

Jacob smiled at me, then down at our son. He spread his lips, wide, showing too-white teeth within amazing beautifully dark skin.

"What are you doing here, Jacob?"

"I just wanted to see my boy. We have many things to discuss, he and I."

"Your boy? You haven't seen him in ..." I stop myself and looked down at my kid. I didn't want to be that person that said all of the horrible things about her child's father. Even though he was an unimaginable evil way beyond what most mothers even fathomed, I still could not say a bad word about the man in front of the boy. To my surprise, our son didn't seem to care one way or another about what was happening now. His eyes focused on his father, but much of the adoration that had once been obvious was now gone. I think Jacob could sense it too. Two years, six months and twenty-six days —no, twenty-seven days, I realized now as I looked at my watch and saw it was after midnight—would do that to anyone.

Jacob took a step toward us, his expression taut as he looked solely at our child. I could tell that he didn't like the change in the boy. No doubt attributing it to something that I had said and not to anything that he had done. Everything that he had done that lead up to him not seeing his child for over two and a half years. I had heard all the rumors, seen the change in the city. I knew what he had been up to. Even probably knew what he wanted. But I would not let it happen. And I was willing to die trying to protect my son. *My son.*

"I have always wondered about cicadas," he said as he ran a hand across his hair. "There are different kinds. Some have 17- and 13-year cycles, some are the annual ones we hear making all that noise throughout the summer. The thing to consider about them is ..."

"Wait ... what? Are you really going to talk about some damned *bugs* right now? Tell me you're joking."

"The thing about cicadas is that although they're suborder, they have huge, lovely eyes that are set wide apart"—he touched each side of his head—"here and here. So that they can see what's seeking up on them. They know ..."

"Jacob, I *really* don't give a shit about any goddamn cicadas."

He laughed. "I always loved it when you got angry. All of that refined education goes straight out the window, doesn't it, now?"

I actually scowled at him. Hated the way that man could get under my skin. "Let's just talk about why you are *really* here."

Jacob could sense the tension. He was always good at that. Truth be told, I was never entirely convinced that he couldn't read my thoughts. Then he smiled. *Smiled.* That bastard. Trying to calm everyone, ease the situation. But it looked contorted and wrong. Everything about Jacob was wrong; I had learned that a long time before. My only desire now was to make sure that none of that wrong would be transferred to my son. And that would be no easy task.

"You've gotten so big since the last time I saw you."

"That happens in three years."

"Your tongue has gotten as quick as your mother's, I see." He sighed. "It's time, little one. You know this, don't you?"

For some reason I didn't say anything; just glanced down at my son who slowly, deliberately, nodded. He knew why his father had come to him this night. It was a damn shame that no one thought to tell me, though, wasn't it.

"No. He's not going anywhere."

"The streets of Harlem aren't safe for a little one like him. You know that, Zee."

"The hell I do. I have been the one here protecting him for all this time. Don't think that I don't know what you have been up to. I hear the rumors, about what you do there in the dark, under the cover of night when no one can see or stop you." He reached for me and I jerked away violently, wanting more than anything to lash out at him. To harm him the way he had harmed us.

"I've been protecting him. I have done nothing in this world but protect this child."

"The hell you have. You left. I stayed. You don't get a choice anymore." I hated saying these things in front of our son, but I had no choice. This bastard left me no choice.

"Red Summer's coming, Zee. And ..."

Before he could finish, my boy was jerked out of my arms. He slid backward, away from both his father and me, as if being pulled by an invisible wire. Or rather, as I slowly realized, something pulled him from within my grasp. Before my mind could process what was happening, I looked to Jacob, silently blaming him.

Jacob held up his hands in surrender, "Wasn't me. You see it's not me."

But, I knew that it could have been. I had seen him perform more difficult tricks than that one. I had seen him move a tree once. Or, shall I say, open a tree, revealing a tunnel into darkness. He got mad at me for refusing to follow him into it. I was angry at him for being who he was.

From the corner of my eye, I saw Jacob dash past me, sprinting for our son. Before he could reach him, he disappeared. Just vanished into thin air. I let out this noise that I can't describe, but was loud and strange and keening. Stood there for longer than I should have.

"Where is he?! Where is he?! Where is he?!" I was talking to Jacob, but unsure if he could hear me. Or perhaps he ignored me because I was babbling. "Where is he? Where is he?" I didn't know what to do, so this was it. Words that seemed to make sense considering the situation, but how could any words make sense considering this situation?

While ignoring me, Jacob stood rooted in the spot our son had disappeared, just staring. Past and through, as unfocused in his gaze as our son had been earlier. He didn't move for a moment and I wanted to touch him, to shake him, to do anything to make him get my son back. But something held me back, closed my lips and muted my fears.

After a moment, Jacob reached into his pocket and pulled something out. From where I was standing, I couldn't tell what it was, but it was shiny like steel, and sharp. It looked kind of like a guitar pick (and Jacob did play the guitar, didn't he?), but I had never seen one that had been sharpened to such a point. Without warning, he slashed the pick across the night sky above where our son had vanished only moments before.

I'm not sure what happened. It was like the whole of the night opened up, the darkness making way for more darkness within the rip. Where there had once been stars as the backdrop, there was merely blank nothingness. Where there had once been atmosphere, there was now a void in the world because Jacob had torn into it as if he was its creator.

I could not move. I could not breathe.

I could only stare as Jacob walked into the rip, the night swallowing him whole.

I stood there alone. The irony had not escaped me. No. I had gone to the finest schools that a bright-skinned woman lighter than a paper bag could ever hope to attend. So, I realized that I had just fought with Jacob about taking our son just to have something else worse get ahold of him. I realized that I had held on to anger for a man who now at least pretended to save our child. But, what if I had been right the first time? What if Jacob had orchestrated all of this just to get his hands on my son. As I waited I got more and more anxious. And angry. I had once trusted this man more than anyone else in my life and he up and left us, without warning. What did he say, he was going for a loaf of bread or milk or whatever the hell it had been. I didn't even remember anymore. Truth be told, I didn't care anymore. My wounds for him had long been callused, but my boy, my boy was the only thing that matter anymore

My boy, whom his father had refused to name, leaving it open for anyone to name him anything. Or, as Jacob had put it, "so that the city could not know him, as he would one day know the city," whatever the hell that meant. I should have asked so many questions, but I trusted that man. Looking back, so much of what he had said to me just didn't make sense, and I never questioned, as if a dutiful little concubine.

I hazarded a step forward, then another. In the spot where the two had gone, the air felt different, charged with electricity somehow. It felt as if I could sense them, but I could no longer see them. In that moment, just as I knew the moon had a pulse, I knew that people exuded an odor to the universe that is unique to them. Perhaps, odor is too strong a word. It was a feeling, a sensation that I could not explain any better than I explained how my son had disappeared or how Jacob had once cause the earth to rumble when he was angry.

I reached out to touch the spot. My hand simply glided through empty air.

What if he had taken our boy? What if I never saw him again? No more riddles about the universe that I didn't understand. No more staying up at night, staring at the ceiling, not telling me what was wrong. No more feeling inadequate as a mother, despite my education. Those thoughts, thankfully, were short-lived.

Suddenly, something grabbed my hand, pulling on me, trying to get me inside the invisible hole. I tried to jerk away, but it was strong and within moments had pulled my whole arm into the void. This was the tree all over again, but this time was different.

I was different.

For a second too long, I thought that I should simply let it take me into wherever it had taken my son. Once I found him, I would figure out how to get him back. So, I surrendered, letting the thing, whatever it was, have me, pulling me further into its world.

I cried.

I cried, but I could not let it have me. I felt so weak, but I struggled pulling first my elbow out and then my whole hand. It held on tight and I decided to pull whatever it was into my world and then beat the—*pardon my French*—living shit out of it.

One hard tug and I pulled them back into our world and time. When they landed at my feet, I saw my boy wrapped in his father's arms and I wept silent tears of joy. I scooped my child up in my arms and held him tight. He couldn't breathe, my bosoms smothering his face, but I didn't care.

"You need to name him."

Jacob looked at me like I had grown three heads. He was panting and his breathing was labored. "What?"

"Name him. You need to name my boy."

"Zee, you're not being rational. I think you're upset. Something impossible just happened. It shouldn't have—I don't even know how it did—but it did happen. I was trying to warn you."

"Name him, Jacob."

"They're after him. They're going to be after both of you. I don't know if I'm strong enough to protect you any longer. I need help." He was almost not talking to me anymore. I'm pretty sure that he thought I had lost my mind, and it is possible that I may have in that moment.

"Maybe Roscoe. I had a friend with that name once."

"Zee, snap out of it. The Red Summer is coming. Everyone can feel it. We can sense it." He shook his head, but not at me. At something that I didn't understand. "It wants the boy. Badly. Do you understand. I need to go back underworld. I have to do what I can to protect him, but you have to too." He stopped talking to look at me. "Do you understand me?"

"Maybe Henry. That was my father's name."

"It will kill him, Zee. Do you want him dead?"

"Momma!" My child shook my shirt, then touched my cheek. "I can feel it. It's strong and bad. I don't like it."

Well, that snapped me out of it, didn't it? "What have you done?" I was talking to Jacob. *I think.*

"Nothing but protect him, I swear."

I stood up, helped my child to his feet. "What do I need to do?"

"Get out of this city. Go to your people. I'll send her to you."

"No. I don't want her around my boy."

"You can't deny her, he belongs to her as much as he does to you."

"That's what I'm afraid of, Jacob."

THERE WAS SOMETHING ABOUT JACOB'S EYES AND WORDS THAT haunted me. Shook me to my core. For all of the smooth-talking, outright lying that Jacob could and did and would do, the look on his face as he tumbled out of the nothingness of that void clutching our son chilled me. He wasn't one to be nervous. This was a man who could rend asunder the very stars. He was afraid. Of what and for what, I don't know. I'm not sure if I really wanted to know at the time. I just wanted it all to go away, I wanted a *normal* child, with normal problems. But I knew that look in his eyes. Same way I could feel the energy in Harlem had been off for a long time. That everything was off. I knew deep down inside me that there was truth to his words. I didn't know what a "Red Summer" was, but I didn't want to stay there to find out.

So we fled.

Chicago's South Side wasn't Harlem, but it was now our home.

It felt familiar seeing so many brown faces, but one in particular was home to me no matter where I was. Jacob had told me to go my people and my Aunt Belle had come up to Chicago from the South, following opportunity like everyone else. The South wasn't good for black folks no more, she had once told me. Not sure it ever was, she followed up, quickly. God knows I wasn't going back down there myself. My mother had come up for school and married well and we all lived well in Harlem when sent me back South for schooling. My mother was convinced that young girls needed to be weaned in the bosoms of Southern charm. Of course that produced the woman you see before you today—unmarried with a son who talks to the moon and an ex who can slash open the night sky.

Maybe the South wouldn't be so bad. Either way, I knew Jacob was right: Harlem wasn't meant for us anymore.

When we arrived at my aunt's little house she showed us to the small room that my son and I would share. It was spare and comfortable and quiet. As I set our belongings out, she stood in the doorway. "Got me a li'l hoodoo shop," she said with a smile. "Nothing much. A speck of a place, but come on and work for me. Family takes care of family and you already know how things go." I took her up on the offer. I knew more about the work than I liked to admit sometimes. I had been drawn to Jacob because he was handsome and powerful. I may not have been able to feel many things, and I was not the worker that my aunt was, but I could sense energy and it excited me—more than my mother liked, of course. Likewise Jacob had been drawn to me cause of mine as well. He sensed the build up in me, the force that I ignored and pretended wasn't there. He said we would make one hell of a pair; that our offspring would be unstoppable. He never mentioned that he would abandon us while having to protect us from afar. I guess some things just don't need to be spoken when you're targeting prey.

Before leaving for work one morning, I was clearing out the breakfast dishes and stopped for a moment, watching my boy stand in front of the front window. As usual, his small brown face was calm, his eyes focused and impassive. I always wondered sometimes what he looks at when he's like that, how he sees the world. "I'm not looking, Momma," he said, taking in a deep breath and letting it out slowly. "I'm feeling. I don't know how you can't feel it too."

"I wish I could, but I can't." That wasn't only partly true. "What are you feeling today?"

He closed his eyes for a moment, drawing in his body as he took another deep breath. Everything about him relaxed as he sighed. "Out there. Everything and everyone out there. I still hear it call your name sometimes, just like in Harlem. But," he looked very sad for a split second and before I even realized it had passed. "Here, something is changed."

"Is it good? Bad?"

"Both. I wish you could feel it. It's real thick like a warm, heavy blanket, but sometimes light like sunshine. Right now, it's like everything is shaking. Not straight. Not smooth. Bouncy. Jittery like when I've had too much candy."

My breath caught at that statement. Things had been feeling different out there to me too, more than normal. There was this underlying vibe in the city. Like a cup about to overflow. I pulled him close to me and hugged him. "I love you, my big ol' feeling everything baby." He laughed and wiped away my kiss.

It was summer, so the boy came to work with me where I could keep an eye on him. Jacob's warning was still scratching around the edges of my mind. I was always nervous and searching. My son was always self-assured and calm so if there was something coming, I started to believe that he would know. We made our way through the streets, passing homes and businesses en route.

"You hear 'bout what happened to that boy?" one man said to another, who nodded in agreement. They were sitting on a stoop, the wooden steps weathered and worn. "Stoned and drowned him. Just for swimming on their side." They shook their heads, faces pained. One of them leaned against the railing. "I didn't come back from the War just to have to still deal with this shit." My son had slowed down some to hear, but I quickly steered him around them as they paused to nod to us. We passed by other men gathered on the street corners. Each of their voices rose as they became more and more agitated, over and over again. We would hear someone say "We need to be ready." My son took a deep breath as they continued to walk. Normally, he liked to walk next to me, but today he held my hand so tight.

"Momma, all of everything is now," he said, his eyes darting back and forth. "Today is crackling." Looking at the tense faces that we passed, I nodded at him. "Yes dear, even I can feel that. I don't like it."

The shop was empty that day, which was a relief. Aunt Belle was out "sourcing inventory and catching clients" as she liked to call it. Which really just meant she was out gossiping and seeing friends and doing readings if folks needed them. I was straightening up some packets of herbs behind the counter when a woman walked in. I could tell by the sound of her shoes that it was a woman, heavier than some, but softer than many. I heard the tinkle of the bell on the door as it closed behind her, and turned around with my usual "Welcome to Belle's!" ready to convince them to buy one of my aunt's concoctions or charms. The feeling drained from out of my body when I saw her.

The woman was short and curvy, wearing a pale blue summer dress with a silk scarf casually tossed across her shoulders. Her matching hat was perched upon kinky-curly reddish-brown hair that was brushed back and pinned up in a loose bun, some loose strands escaping around her face. Golden bangles on both arms jangled as she moved. She slowly sauntered around the shop, touching the different cans and fingering the bags and candles. "My, my ... how *interesting* and appropriate I suppose ..." she said before smiling to herself. "I wonder now, do *I* need to make an appointment for some spiritual work?" She looked over at me.

I remained silent and watched as she walked over to me, hips swinging. It seems like it took forever for her to complete the short distance to me, but man, was she was sight to behold. When she reached the counter, she sat her handbag down between us. A hand covered in gold rings reached down into her full bosom and pulled out a delicate lace-trimmed handkerchief embroidered with a dark blue, calligraphy scripted "J." She dabbed at her face with it, carefully re-folded it, and slid it back down from where it came. "It's starting to become rather hot out there, isn't it? I suppose that is normal for late July, after all," the woman said with a laugh, tapping the counter with a well-manicured finger for effect. The large diamond ring on it glittered. She tilted her head and smiled at me, her hazel eyes appraising me from head to toe. Her full lips broadened into a grin. "Well now, darling, you didn't think I'd find you so easily?"

"Jacqueline," I said, my voice flat. The last thing I wanted to let on was the warmth I felt inside from her gaze. Damn. *So much for trying to lay low. Nothing escapes these two.* "I haven't seen your twin, if you were wondering." She was as pretty as her brother was handsome, and just as sly, only she hid hers better.

"Oh honey, I wasn't wondering at all. I always know where that fool is. Just like I always know where my little piece of sugar right over there is." She nodded towards the back of the shop where he was sitting quietly, reading. "I just thought I'd check in on you. I mean, you didn't think Jacob would let you come all the way out here without someone to look out for you, did you?"

"*Let*? You know what ... I'm already sick of you too. You've got no claims to him."

Jacqueline's mouth twisted to the side. "You sure about that, now? Jacob and I have few secrets between us. We just know that he is *ours*." I glared at her and she laughed again. She waved a hand at me dismissively, the bangles jangling as her many gold rings flashed at me. "Oh Zee, you are still the same. It's been too long. So beautiful. So clever. I missed how unimpressed you are."

"For damn good reason. You and Jacob are just flip sides of the same twisted coin. Like him, your dirt is just as grimy. You just run in a different circle to get yours, that's all. I have to figure out how to protect my son all on my own."

"*Our* son, Zee. Have you forgotten that he is also mine, girl? I gave you your space because you asked me to. I thought I had been respecting your wishes. I did so because I love you. Jacob loves you too, in his own way. We both want to keep you two safe. Don't deny this. You know it is not wise, girl." She looked wistful for a moment. "I came to Chicago because I knew you would be here too." Jacqueline then looked past me, studying the calendar on the wall behind the counter. Her face became alarmed for a moment, as if a revelation suddenly came to her. "It is here. It has arrived here now. Well, that means that we must ... oh, hello there li'l man! Look Zee, he favors me more in the face than Jacob, don't you think?" I hadn't noticed that my son had appeared right next to her. It was enough to make my hackles go up.

"You are like syrup," he said to Jacqueline, his voice somber as his hand made a sinuous gesture in the air.

"Because I am so sweet?" She said, beaming down at him with the same too-bright smile she shared with her brother.

"Because you flow towards things and trap them within it." He said with a shrug. Jacqueline looked at me as I tried to stifle a snicker. The expression on her face suddenly changed from bemusement to seriousness. She reached out and caressed my face. *Goddammit.* Hers was close enough for me to see the spray of freckles across her nose and breathe in the too sweet smell of sugar candy on her breath. I jerked back, recoiling from her touch, and knocked her hand away, livid. Suddenly a familiar rumble in the earth began and then subsided beneath me as Jacqueline sighed and shook her head, muttering beneath her breath. I barely opened my mouth to protest before her attention shifted.

"Well now, would you like to see something special?" Jacqueline said, smiling again as she leaned down to look at my son. There was that charged feeling in the air as he began to nod enthusiastically. *This child is fire and water sometimes. I suppose he gets that honestly.*

I watched Jacqueline as prey watches a predator in their midst. If there was anything I had learned from time with these twin beings is that nothing was assured, they were always unpredictable, and everything and everyone was fair game. And speaking of games ... what was she playing at?

Jacqueline calmly picked her bag off the counter and slid it back onto her arm, as she reached in, pulling out what looked like a shiny, silver mirrored compact. I wanted to scream as I watched my son take Jacqueline's hand, but felt frozen. Something was holding me in place. Jacqueline's own eyes looked frantic for a moment, the hazel now a gleaming green.

"It's here Zee. We feel it. It's here."

Wait ... no, no, no, no, no. Jacqueline stomped the ground twice and I found that I could move again. My eyes widened in alarm as she sliced at the ground with the compact, tearing open a large hole before us on the floor. I knew what was beyond, and like before, I could only see vast, dark nothingness. "I know what happened in Harlem. They are waiting for you my little one. They want to kill what you are. I am not like my brother. I was not going to wait for them to come for you again. I thought that it would be better if I got you myself." She held out her other hand to me, but I could not take it. "I thought it would be better if I got you *both* myself. You've protected him. Now it is our turn." Her eyes. They had Jacob's haunted—or was it *hunted*—look.

"I ... I can't go in there. I can't go in there. I'm not supposed to be in there," I said, as Jacqueline tried to plead with me. It was the tree all over again.

My son looked at me with that preternatural calm of his. "Momma, you have to."

"Your fear of what you don't know keeps you from getting past and seeing what you can do. You tried once, now do it once more. Come on now, damn it! We don't have time for this." Jacqueline did not take her eyes off me as she pulled our son closer. She held out her hand once more.

To me.

This time I took it, gripping it for dear life as the metal of her rings dug into my fingers. It felt like static was running throughout my body. I looked at my son, who looked over at me with a placid face. Unnerved as always. "It is alright, Momma. It's alright. Remember, there is never nothing. Nothing is something too." My child and his platitudes.

And with that we leapt in, the hole above us closing as suddenly as it opened, leaving me only with my screams as the three of us fell together through the void.

Momma.

It's him.

Momma, can you hear me? Can you hear the song?

Soon my screaming stopped. There was no warmth. There was no cold. We were surrounded by blackness so dense that I could see nothing before me. Nothing beside me. No one beside me. The only way that I knew Jacqueline and my boy were still there was because her hand still tightly gripped mine. *My baby.* I tried to call out to him, but my voice made no sound. There was no sound. Nothing. There was nothing but us and the void.

Is this what it was? Is this what he was always looking through? This place that the twins were all too familiar with, tearing open sky and earth alike to travel within it? I had done everything to keep my boy away from it and now the unknown—at least to me—was our destination. Thoughts raced through my mind. I had nothing else but them as we continued our descent. I closed my eyes, feeling the viscous denseness that surrounded us continue to push us downwards.

Momma.

Momma, we have fallen through. This is where the nothing dances. This is where the song comes from. This is where the everything sings. Can't you hear it? Can't you hear them singing your name?

We were there in the dark, in the nothingness, for a long time. Nothing is not simply a lack of light or air. It is the absolute void of everything, including knowledge of one's own body in relation to its surroundings. It is knowing that you exist but not remember how or why or even when understanding that moment of clarity of one's own existence. But the most important thing for you to remember is that nothingness is simply not caring about any of that. It is knowing with absolute certainty that you do not matter in the world. That the nothingness isn't around you, it is, in fact, you. You are nothing.

But that wasn't completely true, was it?

I didn't matter. Perhaps even Jacqueline did not matter, as I could feel very little of her presence as the void consumed my essence. I know one thing if nothing else, however. The boy beside me, mattered. I could feel him as if he were myself. I could not explain in that moment who he was or how he had come to be in this place, but I knew he was integral to everything around me, things seen and unseen.

As my equilibrium returned so did my understand of the world. Then I realized that we were no longer in the void. We had landed, fallen, or rather, a better word would be, we had been "placed" back in my Aunt's shop.

Chicago. Again.

No. That wasn't quite true either, was it? The land, the sky, the life of the city, was all the same. But this was no longer the Chicago I knew. It had changed somehow. It had become something that I no longer recognized. I stood to my feet, my legs feeling wobbly and unstable. Walked to the front door, the bell ringing as I opened, and peered outside. The atmosphere was wrong, too crisp, sweet, like the birth of morning.

It was afternoon. 3:15 to be precise.

"What did you do?" The accusation did not come from me. For the first time in his life my son was unnerved. Angry.

Jacqueline did not look him in the eye as she got to her feet, making her way to the counter again. Her bag seemed lighter some-how. She, however, was unchanged. As I knew she would be, as she always was, no matter the circumstances.

"Tell me."

Still unable to look him in the eyes, she opened the bag. Was that a light within its depths? I could no longer tell reality from my imagination so I did not bother for an answer. None of this made any sense anymore. My son was safe, that was what she had promised and by his response now, I assumed it was what she had given. He was the only one confused by it now.

"Tell me!"

"You are safe. I told you, my son. We could not let anything happen to you."

He looked around, feeling the world around him the way he felt the moon in the night sky. "It's wrong here. It's not the same." I knew what he meant. Even I could feel that things had changed. It looked the same and most people may not have even noticed, but there was something so very different about it. I refused to say, however, that it was wrong as my son had, because nothing about here in Chicago had ever felt right to me.

"It's not wrong, it's an alternative." *What does that mean?* As I wondered my boy shook his head, not accepting his other father's response. She was unfazed, however. "It is between. You will be safe here."

"Between what?" They always talked in riddles. I just needed the truth, for once, the truth. A simple truth.

"Between your world and the under. It's not wrong, like you think it is. It is right."

I did not quite understand and my words were measured, deliberate, as I had only one concern. "In this space, will he be safe?"

"Absolutely." That's all that mattered to me. "And everything will feel the same. The people, the place. You will know it. You can live it out here, until ..."

"No." Our son would not accept this. "I ... I can't breathe here. I need my city. I have to go back, there are things ..."

"No." Jacqueline was resolved. "You don't feel that you can breathe because you were born in chaos. That's all you know. You think you need it to survive."

"I can fix it. I sense what's going to happen. I can fix this."

For the first time she looked at our boy sympathetically, "No, little one, you cannot. You cannot save them from themselves. The only thing you can do is wait it out. The Red Summer does not happen here, in this place, in this time. Yes, it will happen there, but you will be protected from it here."

"Then I die? During Red Summer, I cannot survive?"

"Yes, my son. You die." Her sugary sweet voice became hollow and distant. "It's funny that you call me syrup. You're so much more thick and porous than either of us. You absorb everything around you, adding to it as it becomes larger and snowballs. All of the hatred and anger becomes part of you, until you explode from the weight of it all."

My son refused to accept this. I could not quite tell if he rejected everything she said, or if he simply did not care what would happen to him, choosing instead the violence of the real world over this illusion of safety. His resolve scared me most. I could live out my life in this fake place, with these not quite real people as long as I knew my son was safe and would not be harmed.

"This is not true," he eventually said, rejecting both her words and her, his twin father.

"It is ... not a lie. It's just not entirely the truth, either. It is just other." I did not expect this response. Up until this point, I was relatively certain that Jacqueline had not lied to us. She was like her brother so the truth was relative to her, but she had never openly lied to me. In the past she had been truthful to a fault, telling me of Jacob's preferred sexual positions and too accurate information of his facial expressions during sex, to the point that I believed she was a scorned ex-lover. But the one thing she had never done to me was lie.

"You will absorb the burden of the Red Summer, but as martyr."

"I don't understand." And I didn't. Not at all.

She shook her head and took a deep breath—she could breathe this air without any problems. "Zee, your son—*our son*—is not human. He's not otherworldly like me and Jacob either, but he's not completely human. He's born to alleviate pain, take it on, within himself." She looked down, again unable to meet either of us eye to eye. "We chose you, Zee, because you had the gift. And we expected a powerful child, but not one of him. You see, every generation there is a One born who must suffer and die to cause a shift in things, calm the world, bring about peace."

"He has to die?"

"In order for the world to calm, yes. You feel the tension in the air, like a pot on the verge of boiling? Our son here is the gauge on the stove. He ... he has to be the focal point, the explosion."

"You telling me white folks gonna kill him?" My heart sank to my feet.

She nodded. "He's the right age. He's young and vibrant. Everyone is incensed at the death of the child. They have to kill him. Then they have to get angry with themselves for having allowed it to happen. Then colored folks must resist, violently. Do you understand. Throughout history, only an act such as this will bring about some measure of lasting peace. Until the next generation, that is."

"What is the Red Summer? What is coming?"

"You feel it in the air. Tension, anger, hatred. Things get to a point where hundreds and hundreds of negroes die."

"Can I stop them? If I die, will it stop them?" His face was solemn, determined.

"Boy! ..." I would not hear of it. But they both silenced me in unison, quickly, effectively.

"Your very public death will bring about change. For a while."

"How long?"

"Until they forget what they have done ... Not long for it enough to matter. People have short memories, you see. They don't want to remember what they like to forget."

"Is there another way?"

If I thought the darkness of the void was the depths of nothing, then there was no comparison to hearing the two of them as they stood there in this place that was, yet was not, calmly and matter of factly discussing my son, my boy, my *baby's*, need to die.

My head became like air. Their voices began to sound far away. I heard my son call out to me as I suddenly dropped down to my knees on the ground, my skirt pooling around me on the floor. I could hear nothing more as I placed my hands upon the floor. Inside me, everything was vibrating and when I closed my eyes, I saw flashes of gold and white light. I could feel my hands becoming warmer and warmer.

No.

I refuse to let this happen. *I reject this.* If it does not make a difference then my child does not have to be the sacrifice. Why must it be him? He does not get to be theirs, or the city's, or whatever it is out there that wants him so much more badly than we do or he does himself. I could feel my hair come loose from its pins as I began to shake, my body not quite my own. It felt as if I was drawing from some well within—and drawing deeply. Lifting my hands, feeling the warmth envelop them, and it happened ... so powerful it could not be quelled.

No.

I reject this.

The vibrations were flowing through me, making me feel heady. Some were like short pulses, others like long waves. Some felt like staccato tapping and some like rushing swirls. There was a rhythm and a melody. This was it. *The song. This is the song.* I can hear the song. The waves and light had form, emotion. I was not helpless to its cadence. Each note brought images that resonated to my very soul.

I could hear someone calling my name in the distance, just as my boy had said. It called out to me, singing my name, knowing me just as I knew it. This was so hard for me, I had never experienced anything like this before and I did not know how to handle it now. It was as if this place empowered me, it longed for me to enter, waiting for nothing more than to merger with me. Opening my eyes there was nothing but whiteness. It was crisp and clear. It felt as solid and demanding, and overpowering. "I can hear the song, I can hear the song," I said again and again.

Two strong hands clasped my face and I felt a sharp jolt, knocking me out of my reverie. They were warm and inviting and I knew I had once known these hands like an extension of myself. I once longed for them to touch me in places that embarrassed any self-respecting unmarried woman, yet they had never made me feel shame. After what felt like a long time, I stopped seeing the bright light and colors dance before my eyes and slowly began to focus once more, as the face before me came into focus and I realized that it was not Jacqueline or even my son's, but Jacob's.

"Zee! Zee! Come on now, you have to break free," he said, still holding my face in the palms of his dark hands. "Come on back now. Come on, baby. Follow my voice." His voice, unlike his hands, was silky smooth, deep and full of bass. It was the voice that had trapped my heart, not letting go until I had surrendered both my heart and my virginity. I felt drained, unsteady on my feet and unfocused. I couldn't quite grasp reality, unsure even if this was Jacob. His Essence felt the same, his touch, but I had learned not to trust anything in this place anymore than I trusted the Bulls back in Harlem to give a negro a fair shake. No matter how uneasy I felt, I knew something was off, different. The song had subsided, but it was still there in the background. Or perhaps that was all in my head—I didn't know for sure. Then is was over, just like that, as quickly as it had come. Clearing my head, I noticed Jacqueline leaned against the counter again, bemused. My son ran over, throwing his arms around me in relief. "Momma! You could hear it! You heard it!" I kissed his head and hugged him tightly. "Yes baby, I could hear every note."

I saw Jacob look over to Jacqueline and back at me again. "What do you mean you could hear it, Zee? What could you hear exactly?" I didn't know if he didn't believe me, but I didn't really care what either of them thought anymore. In that moment, I wasn't sure I had ever really cared. They were my child's father, not my own.

I took a moment to look into each of their eyes. "I hear it. Feel it. See it. Deep in me. I understand the song."

Jacqueline looked nervous, her eyes darting downwards towards the floor and then quickly to her brother who did not return her gaze. Jacob tilted his head, one eyebrow raised. Even my son was studying me closely. "What the hell is wrong with all of you? So I can hear it too now. Isn't that a good thing?"

"Well now Zee, that's really something. The rest of us can't hear anything at all here." Jacqueline said with a tap of her kid boots. I looked at Jacob and then my son and they both nodded. "We're dampened in this space. Our abilities have limits when we are between."

"Limits?" My eyes narrowed at Jacqueline. "Wait ... so you brought us here knowing that you couldn't protect us if we needed it?" She merely shrugged and held up a hand, examining and picking at one of her fingernails. I turned to look at her twin. "And *you*, how nice of you to join us? Finally."

"I do know how to make an entrance, don't I?" He flashed that grin at me.

"This is not the time, Jacob." I braced myself against the wall as I steadied myself, rising to my feet. I looked around at the store. Everything looked as it had before, with its pouches and herbs, but something was not right. I could feel it in the song. Something was coming, drawn to us. And it was coming fast.

I walked over to the front of the store and stood before the front window. Thought of my son and took a deep breath, allowing myself to feel everything around me. The vibrations pulsed through me again, but this time, the notes felt discordant and harsh. Every pulse felt jagged and rough, unsettled. My eyesight began to feel clouded and dark as I listened. Instead of warmth, I began to feel a chill, the hairs on my arms standing on end. My eyes went wide. "Can you see them?!" I asked, whirling around, but Jacob and Jacqueline were already standing on either side of me, their faces tense.

"It has found us here too," Jacqueline said, her eyes flashing green.

"I thought I threw it off in the Under ..." Jacob said, shaking his head and frowning as he looked back at our son, who was standing in the middle of the room watching us intently.

"I don't have to die Momma, and neither do the three of you. There is another way," he said and looked directly at me. He simply stood there, waiting.

I looked at Jacob. "Will you name him now? Our son is found wherever he is, even in this space, and he needs a name."

He looked at me as if looking through me. "Zee, when we chose you, we knew that you were special. We knew that you ..."

At that moment, a sound like locomotives, thunder, and an earthquake all in one rushed in front of us. The ground shook and items began to fall off the shelves. Jacqueline and Jacob were unmoved.

I noticed that Jacob had his metal pick in one hand and Jacqueline had drawn out her compact as well. Whatever this was, they knew what it was and were ready. My eyesight went black for a moment and I tried to focus. The darkness blocked the light that was coming through the windows and tendrils began to creep under and around the edges of the door, threatening to open it and pour through.

No.

I reject this.

I looked back again at my son, *our* son, and placed my hands against the door. Took another deep breath and closed my eyes as I drew from whatever was here in this place.

I can hear this song.

And I know how to sing it.

It was then that I knew—this thing, this evil consuming darkness, was what had been pulling at him. This is what had been pulling at my son. It had been the thing to rip him out of my arms in Harlem and pull him into the darkness where only his father could follow and save him. It was the thing that had haunted my son since the moment he was born. The thing that he feared when he called out to the moon at night to save it. This roiling, festering, all-encompassing entity was, I knew with all certainty, Red Summer.

It had been called different names in the past and would be called different ones in the future, but now it was only Red Summer. And it had wanted nothing more than to pull our son to this place where he was at his weakest. We had played right into its hands—if pure evil can have hands, that is.

What it did not anticipate was me.

Zee.

I didn't know how and I didn't know why, but in this place, I was strong.

My son was weak here, more fragile than I had ever seen, but not me. I could absorb this power within this place and somehow use it, harness it, mold it, bending it to my will. I had never experienced anything like this before, not in our space and time. But here, I knew this to be true just as I knew that my child had two fathers, a man and a woman, twins, who had borne him as if they were one.

I looked to Jacob and Jacqueline and instantly they understood without a word from me. I guess that truth was, despite our animosity for each other, we loved the boy more than we hated the pairing we had become. I trusted them to care for my boy. They, in turn, trusted me.

"Go to him, you two! Go to him! I can stop it, at least for a while. Keep him safe. With you he has a chance to go to another space and you can protect him, I know that." I looked back at my son. Jacqueline squeezed my hand and rushed over to him, compact raised. Jacob did not move. "Didn't you hear me?!" I shouted at him. "Go on!"

He held his pick up in the air as the door rattled and banged. "This time Zee, we do this together."

"Jacob!"

"Damn it, girl, listen to me." I stopped, looked at him. "We do this together or not at all."

I nodded and reached out to place my hands on the door, the song loud and clear within me as my hands became warm. I felt the vibration flow out of me.

I felt it all flow out of me. And the world shook. Like thunder rattling the window panes of a house too old to withstand the force, the whole world shook around us. My eyes were closed, but through their lids, I could see brightness surrounding us. Everything around us sounded like the wind whipping with a deafening roar. Behind us, I could hear my boy screaming and my heart sank. Oh no ... Jacqueline had not gotten him to safety in time.

Red Summer was so strong. I could feel the hatred and anger made from fear and panic. I sensed its longing to destroy everything in its path into utter oblivion. It wanted my son simply because it could have him. It wanted the power he possessed. In this world, my son could never be a martyr. In our world, he could never be anything else.

This angered me.

He was a boy. Just a boy. He wasn't to grow up and have a family like every other child. Why did he have to take on the hatred of a world that feared him? Where was he to go? What was he to do to escape the accident of his birth, the pairing of his mother and fathers? How could he not be who he was to the world who hated him simply for who he was? I was furious, blinded by rage against this thing that should not have been. Why did my son have to die?

Is there another way?

I pushed back with everything that I had in me. They could not have him. Not his body that saw what no one else could see or feel or his perfect little mind who dreamt of things that none of us quite understood. They couldn't have either. They can't have him. *They can't have him.* They would not use him and then feel guilt just so that they could forget and do it again to someone else's child. I pushed back. Not my child. Not anyone's child. They would not use us this way. Their guilt did not negate their responsibility. Their hatred had caused this. I could feel it, I could sense it now. Let their children die so that they could abate their culpability. But not ours. Not any more. Not this time.

I pushed back.

Beside me, Jacob and now Jacqueline and our son *pushed back.*

The force of the four of us together was powerful. We worked as one to hold it back, our only goal to try to push it away, to compel it to stop. The weight was so heavy and the burden was so great as it pushed back against us. The song, once sung alone, was now a chorus and every note counted. If we died in that place and time, no one would know. But our son would not carry the weight of their fears or the pain of their false freedom. Our son would not be an example or a martyr today.

Then, as suddenly as it had come, it stopped. There was no more wind. There was no more darkness pushing against us all like a crushing weight. I opened my eyes.

Back home. Chicago. Again.

This time it was really Chicago. *Our* Chicago. No fake place—no in between.

No Red Summer.

It had come and gone through the South Side in the time that we had spent in that place deciding how to react. What felt like hours had actually been a week. In a way, our nonaction was an effective action, but the four of us came back standing in the center of smoldering ashes and charred dreams. I heard our son gasp as he looked around. My own hand flew to my mouth as I looked around us. My aunt's shop, along with nearly a hundred other negro businesses, had been burned to the ground by roving groups of angry whites who did not like that idea that negroes owned something of their own. Even their children joined in the chaos, standing and smiling beside burned out destruction. It hadn't been just us in Chicago, but all over. Hundreds of people, mostly negroes, died.

My son did not.

But it does not matter because Red Summer won.

It always does.

ON VISION AND AUDACITY

There is a certain amount of disbelief when, as a person of color, you state that you write speculative fiction. Whether it is science fiction, fantasy, or horror, that disbelief manifests as a shock about not only the reality, but the possibility.

One thing that we must acknowledge about that disbelief is the root behind it: that we have the audacity to envision ourselves in those genres in the first place.

Whether we identify as African or African American, Asian, Pacific Islander, Native, Latino/a/x, LGBTQ—or any combination of the above—to envision ourselves within these genres means envisioning our very existence. And why shouldn't we? We have always been here, we are here now, and there's good reason to believe that we will be here in the future too. We do not just disappear, which means that it is time to support stories that reflect that.

From within our respective cultural groups, there are stories to be told. Stories that haven't been heard. And there are talented writers more than capable of sharing them with the world. After all, these are the stories we grew up hearing or wondering "What ifs?"

about all of our lives. Now that we have the chance to express ourselves?

It's *on*.

For those who know their reality and what's within it, envisioning a world with us in it is not hard at all. And that reality is a world in which diversity exists and the need to have authentic characters reflecting that diversity realized.

All cultural groups have their myths or folklore or simply want to see themselves represented. Part of the inability to envision has to do with the setting. In fantasy, for example, the standard trope has been protagonists on a journey through pseudo-European medieval landscapes inspired by histories and mythologies that are also European as well. Let's talk about dragons. Yes, dragons. As in knights and swords and fire-breathing ones. There are dragons in Asian mythologies too, but when they have been portrayed in fantasy literature, it is usually a European protagonist slaying, hunting, or taming them.

Another factor is that the publishing world is changing. Thanks to factors such as the Internet, the popularity of manga and anime, and self-publishing, opportunities for writers whose stories may have been previously unheard are now presenting themselves. Viewpoints are slowly but surely beginning to broaden as traditional ways to produce storytelling—as well as who is telling them—are changing.

I want to see us in the future. I want to know that we survive the apocalyptic event too. I want to see us taming, hunting, and being hunted by alien or mythological creatures. I want to see persons who look like us *as* the mythological creatures or magical beings. I want to see us piloting starships across the galaxies. Setting our feet on planets unknown. Using cybertech and bionic implants in a sleek, urban future. Exploring. Battling. Loving. Growing. Learning. Living.

As we *all* do.

We are at a great time to be authors and content creators. The ability to have your work heard and read and seen is more accessible than ever. Go and create.

We're waiting.

-Elle

PUBLICATION INFORMATION

Originally published in...

"Rule of Thirds," *Fireside Magazine*, ed. by Dominik Parisien, Winter 2020/Issue 77

"Roots On Ya," *FIYAH Magazine*, ed. by DaVaun Saunders, Winter 2020/Issue 13; reprinted *Apex Magazine*, January 2021/Issue 121

"With These Hands: A Tale of Uncommon Labour," *FIYAH Magazine*, ed. by Troy Wiggins, Winter 2018/Issue 5; reprinted *Apex Magazine*, January 2019/Issue 116 and in *The Haunted Quill*, ed. by Kate Francia, Megara Publishing, 2021

"Here, Kitty," *Black Magic Women: Terrifying Tales by Scary Sisters*, ed. by Sumiko Saulson, Mocha Memoirs Press, 2018

"A Clink of Crystal Glasses Heard," *SLAY: Stories of the Vampire Noire*, ed. by Nicole Givens Kurtz, Mocha Memoirs Press, 2020

"A Little Not Music," *Sycorax's Daughters*, ed. by Linda Addison, Kinitra Brooks and Susana Morris, Cedar Grove Publishing, 2017

"Breath of Life," *Dark Dreams II: Voices From the Other Side,* ed. by Brandon Massey, Kensington Dafina, 2006

"Empty Vessel," *Dark Dreams: A Collection of Horror and Suspense by Black Writers*, ed. by Brandon Massey, Kensington Dafina, 2004

"What Was THAT?!" *StokerCon 2019 Souvenir Anthology*, ed. by Linda Addison, Horror Writers Association, 2019

"On Vision and Audacity," *Chosen Realities*, Summer 2020/Issue 1, Diverse Writers and Artists of Speculative Fiction

"Hidden," *Chosen Realities*, Summer 2020/Issue 1, Diverse Writers and Artists of Speculative Fiction

"Peregrination," *Chiral Mad 4,* ed. by Michael Bailey and Lucy A. Snyder, Written Backwards, 2018

"VOX," *Apex Magazine,* ed. by Maurice Broaddus, April 2017/Issue 95

"A Place Called Home," *Conjuring Worlds: An Afrofuturism Textbook for Middle Graders,* ed. by B. Sharise Moore, Conjure World LLC, 2021

ABOUT THE AUTHOR

Writer, poet and historian LH Moore's Afrofuturism- and history-inspired speculative fiction and poetry have been in numerous publications and anthologies, such as all three groundbreaking *Dark Dreams* anthologies of Black horror writers; Bram Stoker Award Finalist anthology *Sycorax's Daughters; Black Magic Women; Chiral Mad 4* and *5, SLAY, Conjuring Worlds,* StokerCon 2019, *Humans Are the Problem* anthologies; *Fireside, Apex,* and *FIYAH Magazine*. From Washington, D.C., Moore loves classical guitar, graphic novels, and video games.

ORDER NOW

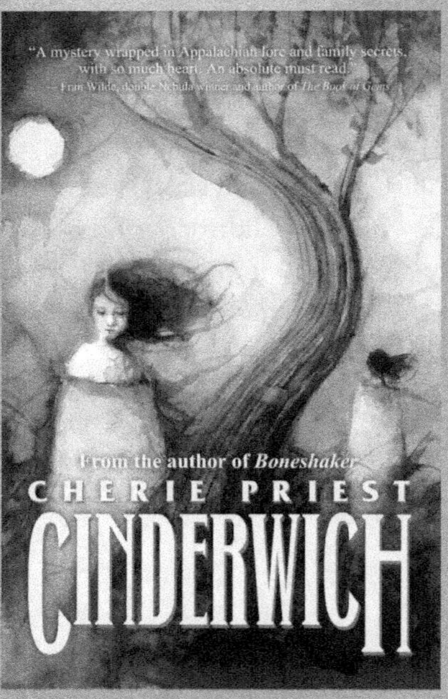

Who put Ellen in the blackgum tree?

Decades after trespassing children
spotted the dessicated corpse
wedged in the treetop, no one knows
the answer.

Cozy horror / Southern Gothic
ISBN 9781955765206
ApexBookCompany.com
Available to bookstores through Diamond/Ingram

9 781955 765299